To Karen –
Enjoy!
Marie Carco

Death – Straight Up

by
Fay Rownell

Fay Rownell

PublishAmerica
Baltimore

ISBN: 1-4137-4194-X
PUBLISHED BY PUBLISHAMERICA, LLLP
www.publishamerica.com
Baltimore

Printed in the United States of America

This book is dedicated to Jim—my soul mate—without a doubt, I am the luckiest woman alive. Thanks to your nightly alarming snorts and soft-palate vibrations—my bold, sweet darling—I was able to lie awake for hours and discover my creativity. Being assaulted by hot flashes and insomnia didn't hurt either.

Acknowledgments

My utmost gratitude goes to my dear mom and dad. You have always been there to support me through thick and thin, no matter what I was up to. You have given me so much more than I could ever have imagined in my lifetime. Thank you.

I would like to give tribute to my "editor-in-chief," my one and only beloved sister Anne. Without you, "Grace," as my role model and confidante, I don't know where I'd be today. You deserve my extreme respect and admiration. By the way, your glasses are on your head.

Noted credit to my personal and patient computer technician and talented photographer, my brother, Paul—I can't thank you enough.

Special appreciation goes to my beautiful sister-in-law, Stephanie, for all your assistance and modeling flair.

I couldn't have done it without all of my other dear family and friends who supported me and urged me on.

And many thanks to all of the staff at PublishAmerica for your patience, advice and giving my first novel a chance.

Prologue

Wipe clean that dripping death
    From tiles icy cold.
    Cold as a tortured mind, whipped.
    Like aged brews of rosehip tea,
    An acrid taste so bold.
    Lamentations, muted in crypt.
    A putrid ulcer none can see.
Expose it all and hold your breath…

Introduction

I awoke that unusually cool May morning—dead. Yes, I said dead. As stiff as a bar order of "make it a double—straight up" and as cold as the ice left out. I'm sure you're contemplating how one wakes up if they are indeed dead. I guess I'd have to say it was more an eventual realization that I had traveled to another realm, but the pure sobriety of my present state was not an immediate reckoning that spring day as I smiled back at the daffodils. As a matter of fact, the final Betty Crocker bake-off was the very last thing on my mind. It all came to light a short while later when I heard my husband Ed shrieking my name. It was only at that point when reality—and Ed—struck me. But before that rude awakening, I peacefully observed Ed in his deepest state of REM sleep. He was more animated in his dreams than our old Labrador had once been, bless his furry old soul. Watching Ed like this always made me smile—I was so very easily amused. Lying there that morning, Ed serenely snorted in and puh-puhed out through his sleep-induced pout. In his abstract state of mind, I caught him forming a hemi-grin, one eyebrow seductively arched. He muttered something unintelligible, most likely propositioning some hot babe, I imagined. In the next moment, he furrowed his brow in rejection and flinched as if he'd been slapped—ouch. Ed was a rugged-looking man yet gentle mannered, his physique and skin healthy—always tanned. I suddenly caught a glimpse of my own skin color. My God, the hue was extraordinary. I resolved I'd get out in the sun today or be sure to put an extra blanket on the bed tonight—or better yet do both.

Wanting some quiet time and so as not to disturb Ed, I quietly made my way downstairs. I gingerly floated room to room, taking in the warmth of the single-framed and collaged photographs of family and friends. I felt I had been so richly rewarded all my life. I silently reminisced about how I grew up in an *Ozzie and Harriet*-type family in a small city where everyone was familiar, quite possibly even distantly related. There was a church and a bar or two around every corner. We used to walk to school as early as kindergarten without a worry. Graduating from high school after surviving my terrible teens, my only goals were to get a job and get out on my own. I had no ambition for college. I was having the time of my life since, after all, this was a time just a stone's throw away from the peace and flower power of the sixties. This groovy era ended when I got married—way too young, I might add, stolen from my proverbial cradle—at the age of 252 months. It was a very poor judgment call that somehow lasted four unfulfilled years, but I did learn a lot about myself and what marriage should not be like. I craved so much more.

So over the next several years I escaped from the only person in my life who didn't believe in me, quit my job and earned my degree in physical therapy. It was shortly thereafter when I found the love of my life, Ed—Ed Lorence—a slightly balding man, in his forties at that time. Sweet, gentle, kind, loving Ed—not what you'd expect from a Vietnam vet. He had been a surgical technician in 'Nam and, boy, did he see it all. When he was honorably discharged after doing his tour, he became head surgical nurse at the local teaching medical center and stayed in that capacity straight through his mid-fifties when he decided to take an early retirement. He had been married for ten years, had no children and, in the process of his bitter divorce, unexpectedly became a happy widower. His inheritance boiled down to a large moggy cat named Maggie, who we strongly believe to be possessed by Ed's ex-wife. Ed and I met through a mix of mutual friends. His wit and the strange workings of his mind stunned me. He could have joined the ranks of Kant, Locke or even

Voltaire. We talked for hours and, though I was appreciating his wit and trying to appear halfway intelligent on the outside, I couldn't help but feel like an intellectual (and politically incorrect) midget on the inside. A dear friend took me aside to boost my sagging self-esteem. *"That's how you learn, Rena!"* I'm sure she was slightly gentler in her word choice and manner, but that was the gist of her advice. I readily accepted Ed's proposals for dating and inevitably for marriage. Ed was Ed. He was so forthright, hiding nothing, telling me every last detail of the events in his life, whether I needed—or wanted—to know them. I had found my soul mate. I could hardly believe we were about to celebrate twenty years of wedded bliss.

After Ed retired from the teaching hospital, he began volunteering at the city's free clinic. Ed had a very large heart—emotionally speaking, I mean. He began bringing home what I affectionately referred to as "strays" from the clinic for a bed and hot meal on a somewhat regular basis. We certainly had plenty of room for guests in our six-bedroom farmhouse. We could have made a fortune running a bed-and-breakfast, but we loved the serenity of our home in the country. These haggard homeless who crossed our threshold became part of our little family.

My career as a physical therapist had evolved over the past two years when I learned of a demand for animal rehab. I supplemented my education with some courses in animal anatomy, physiology and kinesiology. Most of my first year in transition was spent working at veterinary hospitals and animal shelters. I slowly weaned from treating people in their homes to treating animals in the comfort—or not—of their owners' homes. My new patients were hairier and drooled a little more than the patients I was used to—for the most part, that is—but at least they did not complain. I had found over the years that the majority of human patients were insulting, whining hypochondriacs, who wouldn't even know how to loosen up with a Jose Cuervo intravenous. Animals, on the other hand, appreciated any glimpse of human compassion. Their owners, at times, could be amazingly beastly but, over the years with Ed's help, I had learned how to deal with a variety of people. Plus I had an innate ability to elicit trust from all creatures great—and some not so great. I could dress quite casually for work now. I should have stopped wearing dangle earrings, which were especially attractive to cats and birds, but they were the only jewelry I wore. I just added the lobe pulling to my list of occupational hazards. I kept my hair pulled back from my face in a long braid—it was just easier. I noticed recently, though, how my hair seemed to be falling out more than usual, which was starting to make me wig out...

Chapter 1

"Oh, my God. Rena, no! *Rena!*"

'Ed, what the hell is going on?' I was back in the bedroom in what seemed like a blink. 'What are you doing?' Ed was kneeling on the bed and, from my viewpoint, it looked as though he had pinned a large clump of blankets in a wrestling coup. As I came around to face him, I realized that clump of blankets was a body—mine. Ed struck my face with an open hand. My expression was one of frozen terror. 'Ed, stop it! What's wrong with you?' His beautifully tanned skin had faded to pale—panic pale. He shook me violently and I did nothing to stop him. Then he slowly sank back, his hands cupping his gorgeous face. He swung his lowered head from side to side.

"No, no, no," he was sobbing. That was the point when it hit me.

'Jesus Christ, I'm dead! I'm freaking dead. Ed, what did you do? Geez, Ed, in the name of all that's holy—answer me! Oh yeah. I'm dead. I guess you can't hear me.' Shit. This is way too bizarre. I thought I was perfectly healthy, though I guess I had been feeling a little weary lately…

Chapter 2

Because my animal caseload had grown by leaps and bounds, mostly via word of mouth and with little marketing time or expense, my daily schedule had become terribly busy, considering my continued frequent stops at several of the local shelters and veterinary hospitals. My home patients were my favorites, though, and most memorable.

Tiarra Smythe, a self-proclaimed psychic, was the owner of one of my latest animal patients. She was a beefy woman for being so tall, with dye-damaged aubergine hair that kinked all the way down to the top of her plumber's crack. She had a menagerie of cats and their presence was evident before ever seeing them—so, gee, did that make me psychic? There were the fluffed-up, longhaired types that allergy sufferers avoided at all costs, sprawled on tables and countertops with silly names like April and Princess. Then there were the sleek, slim and vocal Siamese types with names like Farouk and Isis. I'm not really sure how many cats resided with Ms. Smythe, nor did I care to know. She had only hired me to treat one in particular named Rapunzel, a pitifully thin Hawaiian hairless. During our initial interview, Tiarra told me that "Punzey" had joined her family of felines about six months ago, but her behaviors had drastically changed over the past five weeks. Tiarra claimed that Punzey seemed depressed and that her present state was affecting the others. As Tiarra devoured one of the largest Reuben sandwiches I've ever seen, she told me that Punzey refused to eat anything and was acting skittish. Plus the other cats were now eating Punzey's food and sleeping most of the time. (I started thinking that maybe Tiarra was the one eating more than her allotted share.) I asked Tiarra if she knew—psychically—why Punzey was so blue, but she advised that Punzey had completely "shut her out" and "all communication was disconnected." My first visit with Punzey was fairly short because she just wouldn't come out from under the bed…

Chapter 3

'That's it, Ed—look under the bed!' Well it was just a thought. I looked too peaceful to have been done in by a lurking monster, but dust-bunny asphyxiation was a good possibility. I peeked under there myself anyway. It made me think of a time when I was only about five years old. The home where I grew up had been burglarized a couple of times and, besides that, my younger brother and I knew that the house was haunted. So I was always a little frightened of monsters lurking under the bed. One night, my arm fell off the bed and my hand settled on someone's face. I was much too frightened to do anything other than hide under the covers for insulation against all evils. No one in my family believed my story the next morning. They all told me it was "just a dream." As I thought about it in later years when the bogeyman didn't scare me (as much), I had to convince myself that it was more than likely one of my older brothers in a drunken stupor. Anyway, those early experiences of break-ins and people on the middle of the floor in the dead of the night—or dead people on the floor in the middle of the night—might have been what initially sparked my unexplained interest in forensic science.

Ed was now on the phone with someone and trying to hold himself together like a tin palace in a hurricane, all seams ready to burst at any moment. The conversation on this end sounded stressed and businesslike and then I realized he had called 911. "Yes, operator, it is an emergency. When I woke up this morning, my wife was dead. No—she's in bed. *Of course* she's still here—that's why I'm calling for help! *How do I know she's dead?* You're kidding me, *right?* She's cold, stiff and won't answer me, *okay?* No, this is *not* a crank call! I don't *need* to take her pulse—believe me, *there* **isn't** *one!*" He gave our address. "Please send someone right away." Ed was speaking in a hoarse whisper. "I need help." He was sobbing again. Apparently, they would send someone and told him it would be at least twenty minutes because of our rural location. Ed listlessly hung up the phone and gently crawled on top of my inert body. He put his head on my no-longer-heaving bosom and cried like a baby.

'Aw, Ed—I am so, so sorry. I can't believe I've done this to you. Hell—I didn't do it on purpose. I'm not really sure what happened. But I do know I'm going to miss growing old with you. Hey, Ed—when you're done crying, could you make sure my eyebrows are plucked—put a little blush on my cheeks—lipstick wouldn't hurt, either—maybe some clean underwear to make my mom happy—before they get here, huh, Ed? And my hair is a mess—would you please brush it out...'

Chapter 4

My second visit with the hairless Rapunzel was much more interesting than the first. I brought soft and chewy kitty treats but kept them hidden from Tiarra, in case she didn't approve. She advised upon my arrival, "I will be in a session with a client while you're working with Punzey. She's a dear woman, I'm guessing in her eighties. She wants to contact her deceased brother to apologize for once having a quick fling with his wife. I don't mean to be priggish, but can you believe that—a lesbian affair with her *sister-in-law?* I told her she ought to just let it be, but she says she can't live with herself anymore. Poor thing—she'll be haunted forever—in one way or another."

Though I kept my curiosity about this psychic business to myself, Tiarra suddenly seized my arm and led me on a brief tour of her reading room, I guess in an attempt to impress me. It was claustrophobically small and dimly lit in an orange haze, adorned with candles, crystals and idols. Tarot cards were on the mosaic-tiled, octagonal table at the ready. The room reeked of incense. The one and only tall, rectangular window at the far end of the narrow room was framed by heavy, brocaded drapes which, Tiarra explained, when closed, held the spirits in the room. Plus she said the added darkness helped her clients to relax. I quickly exited in pirouette fashion before that drapery cord drew my fate in with the rest of them. The old woman soon arrived, decked out entirely in matte black. Tiarra gently escorted her shame-ridden bent frame into the abyss, quietly securing the door behind them.

I sat very still in her living room for a few minutes on the fatigued, sunfaded sofa all shredded like coleslaw from cats' claws, absentmindedly making a few notes about Punzey's history and plan of care. I took a can of chewy kitty treats from my pocket and started shaking it with the hopes of luring her out from under the bed where, Tiarra said, she now spends all of her time. I also thought I'd take advantage of this unforeseen privacy to put my crime scene investigative "skills" to use. This was a silly ritual I had developed over my years of in-home care to make my visits personally more interesting. I was truly fascinated with forensics. I would watch every TV show possible that featured crime scene investigations. I knew, though, that I'd never have the chutzpah to actually make a living out of examining blood splatter, sperm spatter or gaping wounds on the "vics"—I purely enjoyed the fantasy of it.

I scanned the two rooms I could see from where I sat. The biggest offense I could observe at the moment was that Tiarra had never lifted a single psychic finger to clean up around the place or bothered to invest in a maid service. Maybe she figured the spirits would take care of it. I briefly glanced through the dust-matted slats of the Venetian blinds on the front window and spotted a very small, old graveyard across the road. I thought it quite strange I hadn't noticed it my first visit. I was usually drawn to cemeteries and their tranquility. Suddenly hearing muffled voices from the chasm, I cupped my hand around the back of an ear in an attempt to mimic our forefathers' ear trumpets and eavesdrop, temporarily forgetting my purpose for even being there, when I suddenly felt a slab of cold flesh brush up against my arm…

Chapter 5

Ed was vigorously rubbing my icy arm in what looked like an effort to warm and revive me. He was just staring at me incredulously, continually blinking his eyes and shaking his head in utter despair. I felt so horrible about all of this, but what's a poor girl to do? I noticed he was kind of looking through me as if I was transparent, now that my soul had been swiped. He was lost in deep thought. A sudden, loud pounding at the front door made him gasp, inhaling his own saliva, throwing him into such a fit of coughing and gagging that the sheriff's deputy and EMTs at first thought Ed's condition was the purpose of the call. Our recently adopted, old dog was barking ferociously and wouldn't let them come in. Ed, still hacking, had to drag our great protector to his kennel so the men could enter. After they got a blood pressure reading and shoved an oxygen mask over his face, Ed was finally able to say in a wheeze, "It's my wife—she's dead—upstairs—bedroom—don't know—what happened—to her."

They all looked at one another stupidly. The deputy sheriff finally said, "We know'd that's what Mabel the dispatcher done said, but we figgered she got it all wrong when we seen the condition you was in."

They all left Ed alone with his superfluous flow of mucous and ran upstairs, gaping open-mouthed at me. "Wow. She's dead awright. Cold as ice…"

Chapter 6

I had never felt anything quite so nasty. Not only was Punzey paradoxically hairless but the flesh over her scrawny framework wasn't just cold but clammy—Rapunzel was repulsive! Needless to say, she had scared me half to death sneaking up on me while I was so intent on honing my auditory skills. I had screamed, ever so lightly—well, maybe it was ever so louder than lightly—loud enough to interrupt the voodoo session and disconnect their party line with the spirits. Tiarra flung open the door, hands barely able to rest on hips as wide as the jamb, with a searing look of unmitigated disgust. The words "Quick! Shut that door!" raced through my head, but she stood there with it wide open, the matte-black, old lady glowering at me through the opening in the crook of Tiarra's elbow. "Could you please take Punzey into the room at the back of the house so we can have full concentration in here?"

I was so hoping the cheating lesbian's brother hadn't made his appearance yet and escaped the room in a foul mood. I quickly picked up the tiny package of cold, dejected flesh and sprinted to the back room. This was another very small area similar to the otherworldly pit in the front of the house but with den-like decor. There were books everywhere, mostly related to the paranormal, witchcraft, astrology and the like. I cranked my head sideways to get a better look at some of the titles, which also gave some relief to the building muscle tension in my neck.

"See anything interesting?"

I slapped a hand over my mouth to muffle my scream this time, but the resounding opening and closing of my heart valves seemed more than loud enough to wake the dead. Plus, I was sure I now had whiplash. Standing before me in the doorway to this queer book depository was a man—no, a woman—no, I really wasn't quite certain. "It" was wearing men's clothes but they were feminine in color—yellowish pants with a pink, tight-fitting, stretchy polo hiding slight nubs of breast tissue.

"So sorry to frighten you like that. I'm Chris? Tiarra's **man**ager?" "It" now had a name but it revealed squat about the gender. I guessed Chris was fishing to see whether or not Tiarra had mentioned him— her—*whatever*, and I suspected any word with "man" as a part of it to describe Chris most definitely had to be in the form of a question.

I stood there staring, dumbfounded.

"Tiarra probably forgot to mention that I live here too? I'm her booking agent? I set up all her readings *slash* seances and guest appearances at special events?" Every statement ended annoyingly as a query and the voice was so nondescript.

"Oh," I said, snapping out of my trance. "No, she didn't—I mean, yes, she did forget—it must have slipped her mind. Nice to meet you—um— Chris." "It" shook my hand using only three fingers.

"And you must be Rena? The famous animal masseuse I've heard so much about?"

I now imagined that everything about Chris was curious and I was feeling a mite uneasy, especially since I got caught snooping. "Oh, yes, yes, I'm sorry—yes, that's me—Rena Lorence—but I don't really know how famous I am. I'm more a physical therapist than masseuse, though massage is a part of physical therapy." My brain was attempting to warm up quickly, revving like a heavy foot on the pedal of a car with a cold engine. "You'll have to forgive me—I hadn't quite gotten started with Punzey yet—I was just starting actually—just trying to get to know her and her surroundings first." I was in overdrive and, if there were laws for speeding while talking, I would have been nailed on the spot.

"Well, let me fill you in on what *I* think happened to our wittle Punzey." In an effervescent whisper, Chris continued. "Tiarra would just *kill* me if she knew I was telling you this but you need to know. Anyway, Punzey got shut in the reading room one day during a session? She has been freaked ever since, and *I* think she may be possessed? Plus, Tiarra said the session that same day was a failure! Punzey just suddenly stopped eating and playing? She's been hiding under the bed most of the time— she's basically *immobilized*." His, I mean her—oh, hell—Chris' voice had been rising in pitch with each phrase. If there *were* balls in those pants, Chris' legs must have been squeezing the life out of them.

"Well," I said, holding an audible deep breath as I realized I had no clue as to what to do for this terribly sad feline in my arms. Then slowly exhaling and in the most soothing voice I could pull off, I threw it in neutral and purred, "I'm going to do my very best to bring Punzey back around to her normal self..."

Chapter 7

Ed was attempting to calmly explain, "She normally ate breakfast and dinner at home. Sometimes she would bring her lunch to work with her and other times buy it. She usually ate on the fly. Why? You think it was something she ate that killed her?" The coroner had arrived.

"There'th a good chanth, bathed on her color, that it wath poithon," he lisped.

Ed's eyebrows arced, either from the statement itself or the impediment. "Poison! How? Who would do such a thing?" Ed was starting to well up again and struggling to maintain a thread of an appearance of rationality.

"That'th what hath to be invethtigated. An autopthy will be nethethary, Mr. Lorenth."

Miller Sampson, an officer from the Bureau of Criminal Investigation (BCI), had just come in and was conferring with the others. He listened intently to the deputy and coroner's reports with arms folded rigidly in front of him. Miller was a strapping man with serious, dark green eyes. I liked the looks of this guy. There was a hidden charm but an overt confidence in his stance—no nonsense. I felt certain he would figure this whole mess out for us. The din of discussion that had existed among those present for the past twenty minutes had ceased. The room and the overall mood became morbidly quiet and they all just stared at me. Then, seemingly out of nowhere, a deep, yawning voice casually asked, "What's with all the badges?" It was Gus, one of Ed's strays. He had startled everyone, but the sheriff's deputy so much so that he sprayed his mouthful of coffee all over Miller.

"Who the hell is this?" Miller asked sternly, mopping the vile, coffee-flavored spit from his face with the sleeve of his shirt, now forever stained with the memory of this crime.

Ed peered through his curtain of tears and was tongue-tied for a moment. I thought the spectacle might have struck his funny bone, but he kept his composure and finally answered Miller's question. "This is Gus. He's a patient of mine from the city's free clinic. I brought him here last night so he could have a good home-cooked meal and decent bed for a few nights."

They all looked suspiciously at Gus. He was freshly showered and clean-shaven but his straggly, long dishwater-blonde hair seemed to define his homelessness. He was dressed in the same old moth-eaten business suit he always seemed to wear when he visited. He had stayed overnight with us only a couple of times before. I liked Gus. Augustus Freeman was his full name. He had been cast from his home by his wife two years ago after she learned he had lost his job as an industrial hygienist at OSHA. She didn't toss him out on his ass for losing his job. No—that would seem awfully cruel—it was for lying on his résumé. Naturally, she, in turn, had believed everything listed on his résumé was true so she could hardly fathom what else he might have fabricated. The man with whom she shared her life was a total stranger. The little money she had allowed him to have after dumping him and a small suitcase out the door didn't last very long and he had lived on the streets ever since. He was an amusing man—quite charming. I could see how he could easily con anyone into thinking he was someone he was not...

Chapter 8

Moose was a purebred Great Dane who lived with Ralph Walway. Besides the Dane being one of my favorite breeds, Moose was quite simply an enormous bundle of sweetness. Ralph Walway, on the other hand, was a ravenous rogue but before that became obvious, I knew he was a phony at best. I could detect them at any distance. There was a time in my physical therapy career where I was trained to weed out those who were defrauding their employers—the malingerers—those with alleged or exaggerated work injuries. Ralph's claim was that he had been in a hunting accident five years ago, falling from his tree blind and injuring his spinal cord at the thoracic level. He claimed he was paraplegic—almost proudly—like it had always been his life's dream. It wasn't that I disbelieved he fell—though that could have been a crock—but as I observed all of his movements, I had spotted too many inconsistencies. Just noting the muscle bulk of his legs was proof enough that Walway was full of shit as far as his self-declared confinement to a wheelchair. He must have sensed my skepticism as he demonstrated for me at one point that he could use a walker for short distances if he absolutely had to. While doing so, he aspired to make his legs look as paralyzed as possible, pretending to almost throw up with the effort, but the occasional trace movement of the ankle or knee was detected. He was milking the system, getting all the services and all the equipment imaginable intended for those who are faced with real physical challenges. It was sick. And it was sad because Ralph was a thirty-something, good-looking guy—you might even say he was handsomely wholesome—dark brown hair, wide brown eyes set in a round, freckled face. The only thing he seemed to be straightforward about was our discussions about Moose's well-being. Unfortunately, I had witnessed how manipulative he could be with his own home health care staff. It was downright repugnant, but Ralph was thankfully not my problem—Moose was.

And Moose certainly was—well—more of an elephant than moose. He was seven and getting old for a dog of his size—150 pounds, per Ralph's estimate. He clearly had arthritic joints and was in dire need of exercise. Sadly, I thought, 'At least I have something tangible to work with this time.' My first session with Moose, as I decided to do with every home-care patient, was to have a get-to-know-one-another time before starting actual treatment. Though Moose was large and arthritic, he was fast enough on his feet to whip his motion gears in reverse and plop his gigantic ass in my lap before I could do anything about it, which made me laugh right out loud. He certainly wasn't shy—truly an adorable animal—a baby really. And, surprisingly, he and Ralph seemed to have a genuine relationship. Moose had never had his ears clipped and that made him all the more endearing to me. He was a brindle—a mottled ash...

Chapter 9

I was still trying to figure out how to artfully describe the color of my lifeless, hardening skin. It was unlike any person with (politically correct) skin of color I'd ever seen. It was a definite gray but with so many colors muddled in--kind of like one of my early paintings.

Miller Sampson was questioning Ed while the sheriff's deputy grilled Gus. Ed was frantically trying to gather my files to produce a list of my most recent clients. Other crime scene investigation (CSI) crew had arrived and I could see they were photographing me. I also noticed that Ed had not complied with my earlier primping requests—how embarrassing—sorry, Mom. They were processing the scene, looking for the usual incriminating evidence—fingerprints, hairs, etc. I wished so much I could assist. How much fun would *that* be, to investigate my own death?

As they were moving about our bedroom, I suddenly spotted Ed's cat Maggie sitting on my nightstand. I hadn't noticed her there until now. She was intermittently eyeing me as she preened herself, trying to look nonchalant as cats do. I could almost detect a sneer and there was an unfamiliar sound—*damn it!* She was purring! 'Well, Maggie—Ed's all yours once again.' Since the day Maggie and I met, I was convinced the spirit of Ed's ex had taken over that cat. From the start, after Ed told me that she had just had a litter of five, I thought it was wise to have her spayed immediately. Now, most animals took to me like Dr. Doolittle— but not Maggie. After her spaying, all she wanted to do was eat—it was a constant nagging—she never had enough and she never showed any appreciation for what she got. I think that what we spent on cat food all these years was probably what Ed would have ended up spending on his divorce anyway if the proceedings hadn't been so felicitously interrupted. She made sure to get her money's worth. And Maggie would only be playful with Ed but, since she had frequent and extreme mood swings, her short-lived exuberance would suddenly turn to irritation, with Maggie swiping and even hissing at him. She actually drew blood a few times. Ed hated the vacillation. So, there you have it. His ex still had control from the grave.

But what really pissed me off is that I had never, before today, heard that cat purr...

Chapter 10

Punzey had come alive again after only six visits. Initially, the yummies I brought drew her out from under the bed. At first, I found it extremely difficult to show her any affection because touching her rubbery skin simply gave me the willies. I found out on the third visit that Tiarra and Chris had been recently reacting just that same way to poor Punzey. So, along with the strange behavior, she had become unbearable to touch— or vice versa. I brought a little kitty sweater to the next visit and she let me put it on her. She, like most pets, just wanted to be handled and loved. She was transformed into an amazingly cuddly creature, her happy motor running with a full tank of contentment with each stroke of attention. Her trembling, which Tiarra had ascribed to nerves, had subsided. In the end, we were in complete agreement about her overall condition. The season had changed from summer to fall and Punzey had no way of keeping warm other than to shiver. She also stayed near the heat vent, which just happened to be under the bed. Little Punzey had only been experiencing the stark dampness of autumn. And despite assisting her in getting an edge over these obvious physical hardships, I felt I had developed an even deeper camaraderie with Punzey because, no matter what the season, it seemed to me that it would never be easy to feel warm and fuzzy in that house. Thankfully, Punzey had been putting on a little weight from all the treats I gave her and, by the final visit, she was eating normally again. I concluded that the other cats were just getting in their winter hibernation modes and that's why they were eating more and playing less. Tiarra and Chris seemed quite pleased at the sound conclusion of my sessions.

I gave Chris a knowing wink, stating that his earlier theory about Punzey being possessed had been a good one, since I felt our own cat was possessed. After jokingly explaining the suspicions we had about Maggie, Tiarra suggested Ed should try to be more "emotionally supportive" of Maggie. With forehead creased and eyes bugging in disbelief, I accepted final payment for my services. I thought, 'How in the world did she know that Ed's ex had always used that exact same phrase?' I gave Punzey a final pat pat and thought to myself, 'From now on, I'm most definitely keeping Maggie out of our bedroom...'

Chapter 11

I hoped that if I stared straight into Maggie's eyes she would sense me there and freak out *and*—nothing, nada, zilch. No reaction whatsoever. She just lazily arched her back in an upward, then downward stretch—*la de da de da*. She suddenly showed more of an interest in my dead body, though, and cautiously reached out with a paw as if to determine for herself whether I was truly out of the picture. From behind her a CSI agent tried to swat her away, which caused her to yowl and jump five feet in the air, landing on me anyway. She shook all four paws, one at a time with dramatic flavor, to show the categorical disdain for the chill she felt. Ed picked her up roughly and scolded, "Maggie, you're such a despicable cat! I just wish you could be half as warm as Rena is right now!" With that said, Maggie dug her claws in Ed's arm and squirmed out of his grip. Ed let out a yell. "You schizophrenic douche bag! Jesus, I'm bleeding!" CSI stood watching this absurd scene, looking perplexed. Ed started to explain with a nervous laugh how we always felt Maggie was possessed by his ex but, seeing their "is he out of his mind?" expressions, he stopped and said, "Never mind. It was just a private joke we had." When he heard himself say the "had" word, he started crying all over again. CSI told him they were finished.

With an effort-filled grunt, the coroner rolled me over on to a layer of dark, crinkly plastic and said, "You might want to thay your good-bye-th before I thipper her up." Ed slowly bent over and gently kissed my unresponsive, blue lips.

Miller thanked Ed for the patient list and files from the past six months. He assured he would call after investigating the first couple of people. "If you can think of anything else that might have been out of the ordinary recently or anyone you might have the slightest suspicion of hurting Rena, let us know right away." Ed had also given Miller the names of other indigent people he had brought to our home over the past six months but explained that many, if not most, had moved on. Ed added that it had actually been a while since anyone had visited from the shelter or clinic. Gus was the latest. "Well, you never know," Miller said. "Some of these people may have felt you were flaunting your worth instead of appreciating your generosity. They may have gotten jealous to the point of vindictiveness."

Ed looked at him with shock and said, "I have *never* gotten that impression from any of them."

Miller responded with, "Yeah—well, Ed, that's how people end up like Rena—through theatrics and misconceptions…"

Chapter 12

Ralph Walway lived in a second-floor, one-bedroom apartment in a beautifully renovated historic building, circa late 1800s. Though the building restoration did comply with the Americans with Disabilities Act, the original elevator remained. It was so small that it barely held two people at a time, let alone a wheelchair, plus anyone using it had to be adept enough to operate the two manual doors to make it run. It was charming.

Ralph asked that I work with the dog in his bedroom so that Moose could fully relax. I thought the request a little weird at first, but then not *all* that much, since I had worked with many people in their bedrooms for the same reason and for ease of treatment. Ralph advised that he planned to go visit his ailing mother who lived on the other side of town. He felt it would be best if I worked with Moose alone so there would be no distractions. I followed him as he wheeled into his bedroom, listening to him drone on about how his mother is getting old and just can't do what she used to—how he wished he could do more for her—he tries—drone, drone. Then the inflection in his voice changed and I realized he was talking about some girl named Sandy. He was actually telling me how he's not "completely dead" below the waist and that Sandy knows precisely how to handle him, helping him with his urinal, in the shower and, most importantly, in bed.

"Look—I really don't think your sex life is any of my business and an inappropriate topic of discussion here." I felt my face flush in annoyance and, at the same time, I was zapped with a major hot flash. "May I use your bathroom to freshen up?" I began to move in that direction, fully expecting a positive reply.

Instead, overreacting, Ralph swung his chair in a defensive play and blocked the bathroom door, which was ajar. "I'm *very* sorry," he chided. "I forgot to mention that I don't allow *anyone* to use my bathroom, not even my home-care staff. If you need to go, there is a public restroom on the first floor in the lobby. If you just want to wash your hands, you can use the kitchen sink." With that last statement, he sharply pulled the bathroom door closed.

I thought to myself, 'What an *as*shole' and went to the kitchen to splash my face. Here was another room about the size of the elevator. Curious, I asked, "How do you maneuver in such a small kitchen?"

Numbnuts quickly answered, "I don't. That's why I get meals on wheels."

"Leech," I muttered.

"What was that?" Ralph urged from the bedroom.

"I said 'teach'—someone should teach you how to get around in here," I yelled from the kitchen. I realized I needed to control my habit of thinking out loud, but I was just like my dad, who tends to mutter to himself constantly—genetics are pretty tough to get around. I feigned a smile and headed back to start my treatment. Moose was already sprawled on the bed, his huge, rectangular, brick-heavy head on one of the pillows. Yes, I would say that Moose was quite relaxed here.

"I'm heading out now," Ralph advised. "Here's an extra key in case you need to leave and get back in. Otherwise, when you go, just close the door—it locks automatically. Have a good visit. Bye, my Moosey-Woosey. You be a good boy for Rena. Catch you next time."

I watched from the living room window that overlooked the parking lot to observe how he maneuvered getting into his car. He put on a pretty good show—probably expecting me to be at the window. Being that he was on state disability, I figured he must have gotten hand controls for the car—I'd have to slyly check that out before coming up for my next visit. He was driving a rusty, booger-green Dodge Colt.

I quietly sat down on the side of the bed to face Moose. He hadn't even looked up to see Ralph go. Now he was zonked and his snoring sounded like a low, distant rumble of thunder. I figured I'd give him a few minutes' rest and have a quick look around. The first thing that caught my eye from my perch was that the center finial on Ralph's headboard was missing. It was a lovely four-poster antique. I guess the finial could have fallen off ages ago or maybe while telling bedtime stories ol' Ralphie boy had gotten a little rough with Sandy—if there truly *was* a Sandy. Then I turned to look at the foot posts—*WHOA!* Hello—what's this? The posts were not quite straight up and down like they should have been—probably a lot like Ralph. As I inspected more closely, I saw gouges in the wood of each foot post. Hold on—they looked like chain links! *Oh, my God*—what a find! I was really flashing now and figured I'd better get down to the matter at hand—enough CSI play for today—but wow. Now I'd have to try to erase the images that were loosely forming in my brain. Maybe if I could shake my head hard enough, all those little Etch-a-Sketch beads would fall to the floor of my skull.

"C'mon, Moose. Time for your range of motion. Atta' boy." Moose was very cooperative—a great patient. He didn't resist the stretching exercises too much. As a matter of fact, he never even lifted his head from the pillow. His joints were in dire need of WD-40, grinding like sand between teeth with every movement. After the worst of the therapy, I massaged his stiff muscles, gently yet deeply. He moaned in contentment with each rub and gave me a sloppy Moose kiss when I finished. "Now—no overdoing it, Moose. You take it easy, though I'm pretty sure you will. I'll see you in a few days for some more TLC..."

Chapter 13

Ed had called my sister, Lydia, sometime while my life was flashing before me. Lydia was my only sister and we were heartbreakingly close. Everyone could always tell we were sisters, not only from our looks but our voices. We sounded almost identical and had even fooled family at times. We always joked that we were actually twins, just born four years apart. She arrived just as the coroner and gang were hauling my zip-locked body out the door. Lydia came unglued when she saw the bag and requested that I be brought back inside. The coroner reluctantly agreed and said, "I do underthtand thith ith your thithter. We'll give you a few thecondth to be with her." Lydia looked at Ed for a moment wide-eyed. As they unlocked my freshness, the coroner said, "Pleathe prepare yourthelf."

Lydia almost fainted when she saw my color. Ed put his arms around her before her knees gave way and let her get it all out. As Ed handed her a tissue to blow her nose, she noticed the streak of blood that had coagulated on his arm and hand. "Oh, my God, Ed—you're bleeding," she cried.

"Oh, that was just Maggie's retaliation to an insult I gave her," Ed pooh-poohed.

"I wish you'd get rid of that cat—she spooks me! You need to wash those cuts out." Lydia began to leave the room to get the peroxide, almost forgetting about my lifeless lump. "Oh, I'm so sorry," she said to the coroner. "Please—go ahead—I know you have your job to do."

"Thankth…"

Chapter 14

Tiffany Duffer just couldn't seem to thank me enough when I told her I would stop by the next day to evaluate her cockatoo, Tweaker. She had learned of my services and gotten my name and number through Tiarra Smythe. Tiffany briefed that Tweaker's main problem was that he couldn't walk. She also advised that his crest was no longer erect. I asked how long she had owned Tweaker and whether or not he ever was able to walk. She said she had him now for a couple of months and that he did initially walk in the store and in his cage. He spent most of his time now, though, on her shoulder. If he flew to the floor, counter or furniture, he would just freeze and usually just fly right back to her shoulder. I really knew nothing about treating birds, especially how to rehabilitate a flaccid crest, but thought I might as well give it a shot.

Tiffany answered the door to her dinky mobile home—topless—Tweaker in tow.

"OH!" I blurted. "My—what a beautiful bird," trying not to let my eyes be diverted. My peripheral vision forced me to determine, however, that she had been harshly manipulated by earth's gravitational force (among other things). I promptly guessed she was probably only in her forties but appeared quite frayed around the edges, like an old favorite sweatshirt. Her black roots had unearthed and were screaming for more Clorox. I hate to think poorly of anyone at first glance, but my first impression of Tiffany Duffer was snake-belly low.

"I hope you can help my Tweaker," she squealed in her supplicating way. "I'm so worried for him, especially since his crest went limp."

I briefly pondered how he came to be dubbed Tweaker. "Well I sure hope I can help him too. May I come in?"

Tiffany hesitated, looking anguished and with a scrunched brow said, "My house is such a mess—I hope you'll forgive me. I just haven't had *any* time to clean up."

As I entered, my stomach performed a triple gainer. Not that the place smelled all that bad, which was pretty amazing in and of itself. It really just smelled like deep-frying oil. What got to me more was the clutter. I thought, 'Tiarra Smythe was immaculate compared to this one.' There was literally not one inch of space on the monkey-shit-brown shag carpeted floor to walk, on the orange-and-avocado-flowered furniture to sit or on the heavily stained formica counter to put my bag down. I excused myself for a moment and ran back outside to put my bag and jacket in the car. A few deep breaths later, I re-entered. This time, from across the room, there was no way I could avoid it—I looked straight at them. Her breasts were gargantuan and hung clear to her navel. Her nipples alone were the size of dinner plates.

"I know you must think it strange that I'm topless but I'm really most comfy this way. I'm a former exotic dancer, you know." It was more a proclamation than an expected confession or apology. "I was sadly let go when a new string of younger dancers hit the scene—just my luck."

She was let go, all right. "Gee, that's too bad—I think." I was almost stuttering, both from disgust and her unabashed stupidity. She was a complete boob—*literally*—especially if you squinted!

"Well, come on over and take a look at Tweaker while I start dinner."

I stumbled across the room, stepping on papers, magazines, clothes, videos, pots and pans, food remnants, shoes, throw pillows, dishes—you name it—just trying to focus on the task at hand. I certainly didn't want to trip and fall into that garbage heap on the floor—or worse. I kept at arm's length away from Tiffany and put my finger out for Tweaker to perch on. I was surprised he came to me so willingly. I stroked his gorgeous salmon-tinted feathers as I looked for a spot to sit. Triple D cleared a chair for me by tossing the contents of the chair on the floor—wow, what a surprise. I made sure not to sit all the way back for fear of sticking. I only wanted to do my assessment with Tweaker comfortable on my lap and then get the hell out of there.

"You know," Triple D cautioned, "I have a friend who could probably use your services, too." I looked up to see Tiffany standing at the stove, her flesh way too close for comfort to the frying pan.

"You really ought to be careful over there—you're going to burn yourself."

"Ooh," she annoyingly giggled. "I do that all the time. My bazooms seem to always get in the way! Once they went right in a pan of hot grease. My sweetie Marvin was so worried. He slathered petroleum jelly on them—the blisters healed—eventually."

Now I felt I had just belly-flopped from the high dive—my stomach was in spasms. 'Deep breaths, Rena—concentrate.' I closed my eyes tightly a moment to meditate, turning away from the greatest visible contradiction the marketing team for Playtex could ever imagine. I needed to re-focus on Tweaker.

"Has he lost his appetite?" I innocently asked, feeling that mine would be gone for all eternity.

"Who—Nick? No, he's okay—he wants you to look at his Butchie."

"Who the fff—um, who's Nick? I was asking about Tweaker." Any minute now I expected Rod Serling to appear—or Alan Funt.

"Ohhhh," she grated. "I was talking before about my friend, Nickie. He thinks you could help his Butchie."

My brain hurt. If she were any less intelligent, she'd be a rock. My patience was waning and I was a little anxious over who or what "Butchie" was. "Just tell your friend to call me for an appointment."

"Does he have your number?" she had the nerve to ask.

"No, Tiffany—but you do." My curiosity got the best of me and I just had to look back over toward the stove. "Why don't you just wear an apron when you cook?"

"What a *great* idea! I can't believe *I* never thought of that!"

God help me, I prayed. How could I have even thought of insulting a rock like that? Her brain was translucent—non-existent really...

Chapter 15

The coroner decided it was time to get me out of the house before I released any more staleness. He zipped me securely in what I'm sure would be considered the latest line in fashion designer body bags, whisking me off to the morgue. Miller Sampson decided he would escort Gus to the local shelter and probably grill him further on the way. I had the feeling his confidence in the deputy sheriff's intellect and interrogation skills was lacking. Plus their relationship hadn't exactly had a clean start.

"So what happens now?" Lydia asked Ed.

"Well, I guess we just let them do their jobs and wait for their findings."

"I can't just sit around and wait, Ed. I'll lose my mind. I think we should do some investigating of our own." Lydia was shaken beyond belief and knew she couldn't just sit around in a daze waiting for an answer. "The coroner told you it might be poison, so I'm going to research poisons on-line. Maybe you could try to talk with some of her clients. I know she mentioned there were some screwballs in the pack."

"No," Ed pointed out. "The coroner didn't say it 'might be poison.' He advised and I quote, 'There'th a good chanth it wath poithon."

Lydia shot Ed a look as if to say "How dare you!" but caught the familiar gleam in Ed's eye and they both burst into laughter. They laughed until they cried and cried until they laughed again. Half a box of Kleenex later, Lydia gave a final blow in her tissue and stuffed it in Ed's shirt pocket. They were both exhausted from the day, eyes red and swollen. Lydia sighed, "Let's have a drink—a real drink. We'll get a fresh start in the morning."

Ed agreed. "How 'bout a Manhattan and some comfort food—something cheesy…"

Chapter 16

Nick Fagioli (pronounced like the pasta-bean dish) was a grease monkey at Marvin's Automotive. He called me the night after I saw Tweaker and asked if I could try to help their twelve-year-old teacup Chihuahua, Butch. Nick explained that Butch had fallen from his wife's shirt pocket and broke a leg about six weeks ago. He had just had his cast removed and needed help with moving the leg again.

Their last name reminded me of an experience I had years ago with an Italian patient. He had fixed this pasta fagioli dish for me and was in the process of dictating the recipe to me, when I asked how to spell "fagioli." He said, "I dunno—FA—ZHULE"—not spelling it out, just using phonetics. I had a good chuckle to myself, but I had to admit that while he was deficient in orthography, his cooking was superb.

Nick answered the door when I arrived the next day. I was astounded with his stereotypical dark and handsome looks, just minus the "tall." He was pleasingly pumped, his biceps bulging from the rolled-up sleeves of his dirty, faded-to-almost-purple, blue mechanic's shirt. Nick, as the red and white name tag indicated, had taken time off to meet me for my first visit and further explain some of Butch's history.

"Ya see, Butchie here has quite da strong attachment to da wife—HEY, JAMIE! GIT YER ASS OUT HERE AND MEET YER NOICE! My James and Butchie was just restin' in da udder room. C'MON! MOVE IT!"

"Actually, Nick, I'm not a nurse. I'm a physical therapist."

"Yeah, yeah—whateva. All I know's is dat you's gonna help little Butchie git betta. Here's da little guy now. Butchie—say hi ta da noice."

Butchie's little head was all that was showing from the wide pocket of Jamie's shirt. His pointy ears seemed too large for his head. I introduced myself to his wife, as I could see Nick was never going to refer to me as anything other than Butchie's "noice." His wife was gorgeous but painfully shy. She had very short, dark hair and dark, almond eyes— Sophia Loren eyes. Nick explained that Butch always traveled in Jamie's pockets and didn't take much to strangers. The problem, though, was that they were afraid they'd hurt Butchie with the exercises recommended and were advised by the vet to call in a pro. I asked Jamie to take Butchie out of her breast pocket so I could try to evaluate his condition. Jamie advised me, in an almost inaudible voice, "I don't think Butchie will come out until he gets ta know ya betta. He'll let ya pet him as long as he can stay put." I warily reached over, letting Butchie smell the back of my hand, which had a dog treat hiding in the palm. Once he gave me a lick of approval, I rewarded him and gently patted his head.

Nick exclaimed, "WOW! Wouldya look at dat," and then ordered, "Why dontcha stick yer hand in da pocket and woik yer noicin' magic."

I looked at Jamie questioningly and she nodded her permission. Now I'm thinking, 'Great. I get to feel her up at the same time, while lucky Nick here gets to watch.' I reached in tentatively and felt Butchie's legs. Three of them were quite limber and one was very stiff—which is how I pictured Nick to be right about now. I was horrified to look his way since I had noticed he was breathing heavily—slack-jawed. I happily noted, though, that Jamie had extremely small breasts and so I literally didn't feel anything I was doing was improper.

"I'm never going to be able to effectively work Butchie's leg while he's in your pocket," I told Jamie. "Maybe I could stop by again tomorrow and we could work with him on your lap instead. I think he'll comply now that he knows me."

Jamie didn't have time to respond as Nick surprisingly jumped in with, "Yeah, yeah—sounds like a plan." I didn't expect that he'd want today's show to end so soon. "I won't be able ta take no more time off, dough, so just let James know what time yous'll be comin'. I gotta get back ta woik now anyways." Nick donned his dark mustard-brown Carhartt jacket and walked out the door. A small feather fluttered to the floor. I thought it must have dropped from my bag and so casually picked it up and threw it in the wastebasket. Jamie never even noticed. She was too busy waving to Nick from the doorway. I felt so sorry for her. I wondered if she ever got to confide in anyone about her problems. I wondered if she had a sister...

Chapter 17

Lydia had multiple computer printouts of various poisons and their effects strewn all over the living room floor, studying each one very carefully.

The night before, she and Ed drowned their sorrows with several stiff drinks and a dinner of grilled cheese and tomato soup—Ed's specialty. They discussed plans for my remains, with Ed explaining how I didn't want to be buried or have any church service. Even though I had been raised a Catholic and attended parochial school through the eighth grade, as the tide of my maturity rose, my faith in Catholicism ebbed. I would be cremated and Ed would throw a big party for family and friends to celebrate my life. They would have a ceremonial disposal of my ashes, some to be scattered in our pond and the remainder in my flowerbeds. Lydia had phoned the rest of the family to give them the gruesome news. She told my parents in Florida to just stay put for now. My dad was now ninety-one and my mom eighty-four. Lydia said she'd arrange their flight up for them soon. Naturally, they were beside themselves. My three older brothers, who lived in various parts of the country, were astounded and didn't quite know what to say or do. Lydia told them there was really nothing for anyone to do but wait for the coroner's and investigative findings. Then they could arrange for their final good-byes. My baby brother, Blake, on the other hand, shocked Lydia when he blurted, "I knew it. I knew something happened to Rena. I had a dream last night that she was suffocating or drowning—she was paralyzed and couldn't signal for help." Blake's throat tightened and he said, "We've always had a special sort of telepathic connection—it was eerie—I should have called Ed." Blake and I, though we fought like crazy as kids, had become very close as adults. He had been such an apple-cheeked cutie as a boy. He really hadn't changed much but the cute had turned to downright handsome.

"Oh, c'mon, Blake," Lydia tried to reassure, "it was only a dream."

"Was it?" Blake was sniffling on the other end of the line and Lydia told him to go get some rest—she'd call him later.

While Lydia continued with her research, Ed decided he would stop by the BCI office to check on their progress and to see if he could assist with their inquiries. Ed had given them all of the names of my most recent clients. He told Miller he would speak with the clients he knew I had loved and trusted, not only to advise them of my demise but also to ascertain any information I might not have shared with him, though Ed assured himself and Miller that we had no secrets. Ed figured he would stop by today to see Dom at the bakery and pick up a loaf of fresh bread while he was at it…

Chapter 18

Dom Modigliani called me for an appointment to evaluate his Jack Russell, Geyser. With a thick Italian accent, Dom sadly reported that his wife had recently been killed in an attempted armed robbery and said their dog was injured at the same time. I could hear Dom was terribly shaken and suggested he wait to explain the entire incident to me when I came for my first visit.

Dom's bakery was a family business that had been in operation for generations. Dom was now in his early eighties but still helped his sons run the place. Dom was a robust, old-worldly kind of a guy for his years but, uncharacteristically, dressed in disco-esque pastel polyester. He lived in a large apartment over the bakery filled with a charming character associated with the architecture of older homes. During our first visit together, I fell in love with Dom immediately. He was such a huge mix of emotions—one moment tearful and singing a little "O, Sole Mio" and in the next moment bursting into hearty laughter. Before I had a chance to evaluate "Guy," as Dom called him, he insisted I join him at his table for a bite to eat. I couldn't argue because the aroma wafting up from the bakery had my stomach juices flowing like Niagara Falls. He warmed up enough lasagna and greens to hold me for a few days. After we ate he showed me to his den, where the antique mahogany furniture possessed a warmth that equaled Dom's persona. He left me for a moment and returned with espresso and a cannoli. Dom settled on the opposite end of the red tufted leather chesterfield where I waited and heaved a sigh.

"A cuppa two-tree weeks ago, my wife, Gina—my Gina—was'a workin' to help wait on'a da customa. It was a fairly quiet affatanoon'a. My son'a, Tony, was in'a da back'a, bakin'a bread'a. Out'a nowheres, a man'a come in'a, pointed a gun right at'a my Gina—da security camera caught it all'a. It looked like he was'a demandin'a money but Gina—my Gina—bein' an old, stubborn Italiana was'a wavin' her hands anna' yellin' at 'em to git out'a. Our dog'a, Guy, he was in'a da store wit'a Gina anna' he come runnin' out'a from'a back'a, bitin' at'a da man's leg'a. Da man'a tried'a kickin'a Guy, but'a Guy had a good moutaful'a. Dis'a man'a pointed'a gun at'a Guy but Gina—my Gina—she come round anna' trew herself at'a da man'a. He pointed'a gun at'a her—he shot'a my Gina." Dom paused to collect his thoughts, stood up and wearily walked across the room to an old, hand-carved hutch. He brought back an etched, silver tray carrying two exquisite liqueur glasses and a decanter of Sambuca. With trembling hands, he carefully placed the tray on the glass top of the ornate coffee table. Dom looked at me pleadingly with teary, bloodshot eyes. "Have a drink wit'a me'a?" I nodded my consent and he poured. "Salute."

After a few more moments of silence for his Gina and a second pouring of 'buca, Dom continued. "My Gina—she was'a kilt instantly—one'a bullet in'a da head'a. Guy, he letta' go of'a da man'a, runnin' to'a my Gina. Gina fell'a—landin'a smack on'a our little Guy. Twas a miracle Guy was'a not'a kilt too'a. My Gina—she was'a big'a woman—at least'a tree-hundred pound'a. She was quite'a cook'a—my Gina—oofa! Too bad she didn'a land on'a da man'a—jus'a squash'a da creep like'a bug'a. Anyways, our little Guy he suffer some sprain anna' strain'a. He not' doin' too bad'a—considerin'—but I taught'a some'a professional type'a care would'a be good for our brave'a boy'a. You wann'a to meet him now'a?"

"I would love to meet that brave little boy now, Dom. I just want you to know how terribly sorry I am for you and your family. It's so tragic. Did they ever catch the man who did this?"

"No, not'a yet'a. After he shot'a my Gina, he ran'a—never even stole a dime'a! I don'a t'ink he ever meant to use'a his gun'a. Guy was'a just tryin' to protect'a my Gina. If only she had'a fallen on'a dat dirty sonofabitch—dat would'a been'a sometin', huh?" Dom wiped a tear and gave me a mellow smile. "I'll go get'a Guy now'a."

We stepped out into the main living room and Dom descended the back stairs to the bakery, calling out for Geyser. Glancing around the apartment I quickly observed there was not a thing out of place. Besides Gina's murder, the tacky furniture still covered in plastic was the only crime here...

Chapter 19

On the way to the homeless shelter, Miller Sampson and Gus Freeman had an enlightening discussion. Gus shared the fateful events that led to his being on the streets.

"So why the hell didn't you just get a job you were qualified for?" Miller asked. "Why would you throw away your life like that?"

Gus gave a long, drawn-out sigh. "I don't know—I was cocky—overconfident—thought I could put one over on anyone—an entire federal organization for that matter. I've done it all my life, Miller. Guess I never really thought human resources would go so far as to do a background check with the colleges I listed."

"Well what about your wife? How could you scam someone you loved?"

"I did love her, you know—still do. I guess I just have never liked my true self—never thought anyone else would either."

"So, Gus—who is your 'true self?'"

"I'm not sure anymore, Miller. I've told so many lies all my life, I think I've lost that person."

"What did you do before you worked for OSHA?"

"I was in and out of college—did odd jobs. I had always been a roamer. I met my wife on campus. This job with OSHA had been my longest employment. I had them fooled for a full year. Guess I started fucking up on some of the more technical bullshit—that's when they got suspicious of my educational background. Yeah, the longest I had stayed in one place, one job—and married, for that matter."

"Oh? You were married before?"

"Yeah—only for about four months. That was one of the only times I *did* reveal my true self and my wife couldn't stand me, so we had the marriage annulled and I moved on."

"Why did she marry you in the first place?"

"I think she felt sorry for me. I was alone—pretty pitiful. No family to speak of. It was a mercy marriage."

"What do you mean 'no family to speak of?'"

"My parents are both dead and gone. My one sister, Corinne, is out there somewhere. We both moved away from our hometown after our folks passed on. The last time we spoke was three years ago and she was getting ready to move again, so I have no idea where she is now."

"Where did you grow up?"

"Everywhere—anywhere—you name it."

"No, I mean where were you born? You must have lived in one place for a while as a child?"

"I was born in Mission Ridge, South Dakota, but we moved a lot."

"I'm sorry—sounds like you've had a pretty tough life all in all. What are you, say about forty-five or so?"

"Yeah, somethin' like that."

"How often did you go to the Lorence home?"

"This had only been my third time. What a great guy Ed is. It's really so sad about Rena, huh? They sure seemed happy together. I couldn't believe their generosity."

"So, you don't think Ed had anything to do with this then?"

"Hell, no. They had it all. Why would he want to go and ruin that?"

Miller questioned Gus about his activities at the Lorence home the night before. Gus claimed he went to bed after eating and drinking much more than his usual—Rena was the last one up. Gus didn't seem suspect, but didn't plan to rule him out completely either. "Do you know any of Ed's other patients who might have been brought out to their home for an overnight stay?"

"Yeah, but some have moved on. One lady I know of—last name is Looby. She's still around and what a hoot. She talks up Ed all the time—almost obsessively. She seems harmless but her mind is going, though—repeats herself a lot. Probably from all the boozing…"

Chapter 20

I received a call from Marvin's Automotive one morning around seven-thirty, just as I was stepping out of the shower. I ran to get it, hoping it might be a cancellation in my schedule.

"Uh, yeah, hi. Is dis da noice?"

In a lame attempt at humoring myself first thing in the morning, I wondered, 'Gee—who could this smooth, articulate man be?' so I said, "This is Rena—can I help you?" Then I thought I probably shouldn't play dumb—what a turn-on for him.

"Uh, yeah, hi," he says again. "This is Nick—Nick Fagioli?"

"Yes, I know, Nick."

"Uh, yeah. I was wond'rin'—wouldya be able to see anudda customa today? It's my boss, Marvin. He's got some pet dat needs lookin' at."

"Today? No, Nick. I have a full schedule today. Can he wait a day or two?"

"Uh, no. He's takin' today off and he says he just wants a noice ta examine his sick pet."

"Okay, Nick—I'll see what I can work out."

"By da way—uh—Butchie's comin' along real nice. He's even bein' friendly and all."

"Thanks, Nick. I'm glad you're satisfied with my services."

"Uh, yeah. Yer da noice of da year!"

I allowed Nick to proceed with his eloquence for another nanosecond, then got the necessary information to make an appointment. I arrived at Marvin's place around 5 p.m., after a full day at the local animal shelter. Marvin lived in a motel rental, which came as a surprise for the owner and operator of what appeared to be a solid business. I was beyond tired, suffering from sensory overload from the incessant yipping and heart-wrenching feline pleas. The shelter odors had permeated my nose hairs and my tailbone ached after being knocked to the ground by an over-enthusiastic boxer mix that thought for sure I was there to post bail. It took several minutes for him to respond to my knocking. I was not in the mood to be held up any longer than necessary from sipping on a martini and melting away the day in my hot tub. He opened the door slowly, peering through squinted eyes.

"Hi. I'm Rena. Are you Marvin?"

"Yeah. C'mon in. I've been waitin'." His words sounded like they had been led on a misguided tour, escaping through his nasal passages.

A cloud of second-hand cigarette smoke consumed his one-room motel apartment, strangling the last breath of clean air in my lungs. The walls were stained the color of bladder-infected urine, as were Marvin's remaining teeth. His heavy breath reeked of cheap rotgut. In the dim light of this cubicle he called home, I could see his thinning hair was as greasy as any well-lubed engine he'd recently serviced, and his pocked face resembled Goodyear's finest treads. His wrinkled mechanic's uniform hung loosely from his scraggy body and was saturated in offensive odors.

"So, Nick said you needed me to come over here—*today*—to see your sick pet. Where is it?" I was beginning to feel enormous displeasure as Marvin ogled me in a splayed stance not unlike a newborn wildebeest, swaying to some unheard melody.

"Oh, yeah—right this way." Marvin led me a whopping fifteen feet to a corner of the room where a small fish tank sat on an end table. "It's my tetra here—he's been actin' kinda funny." Marvin was smirking at me, his eyelids at half-mast, trying to look suave.

"Listen, Marvin. I don't find this one bit amusing. You are wasting my time after a very long and stressful day. The request for this visit was fraudulent. Now I am just completely exhausted and totally pissed off."

"*Whoa*—those are pretty big words comin' from a nurse."

"I'm *not* a nurse! I'm a physical therapist who specializes in animal rehabilitation. Animals, Marvin—not *fish*!" Not only was I angry about this farcical set-up but downright nauseous from the coalescence of pervasive odors.

"Hey, baby—don't be mad. I thought maybe once you were here, you'd warm up to ol' Marvy and maybe give me one of your special nursin' rubdowns."

"I am *not* your baby! And you tell your friend Nick that I didn't find this amusing at all!" I headed straight for the door, but Marvin's grimy mitt caught my arm.

"C'mon, nursie. Don't go yet."

Without any thought, I propelled my arm to break his grip and shoved him with the rush of adrenaline that now coursed my blood. In his current condition, I probably could have just blown him out like a candle, but I gave it all I had. Marvin's feet literally left the floor and he landed on his ass, knocking into the end table, the fish tank spewing flip-flopping guppies and tetra everywhere. Marvin probably hadn't had a bath, at least quite like this one, in a long time. He was stunned, shaking his head in what looked like an attempt to just clear his vision. 'Poor fish,' I thought. 'They'll probably all die—now *that's* a crime.' As I opened the door to leave, I realized that Bugs Bunny was on the TV. I laughingly looked at Marvin and said, "B'dee, b'dee, b'dee—that's all folks!" and walked out, leaving him befuddled in his own cartoon scene...

Chapter 21

"Hello—Mithter Lorenth? Thith ith Thtanford Thtefanik—the coroner."

"Yes, Mr. Stefanik—do you have any news?" Ed pleaded.

"Pleath—call me Thtan."

Ed paused a second—hmm—but then said, "Okay, Stan. What have you found?"

"Firtht, thith ith going to take longer than we ever eggthpected. Rena'th inithal blood work thowed multiple chemicalth. We want to thort through every latht one of them to determine the eggthact cauth of death."

"Multiple chemicals? What kind of chemicals?"

"Variouth one-th that are uthually found in inthectithide-th, herbithide-th and rodentithide-th. Do you know if you have theeth typth of producth around the houth?"

Ed's head shook in such total disbelief that he looked like he had suddenly developed essential tremors. "I just can't believe this! Rena loved to garden, but she is—I mean was—an organic gardener. She never used any chemicals in the garden. And, did you say rodenticides? You mean poison for rodents?"

"Yeth, Mithter Lorenth—rodenth."

"Please, Stan, you can call me Ed and, no, we don't have anything like that. Our cat is the only rodent killer here."

"Well, Ed, there were many different compoundth found in her thythtem which we would like to thtudy further. We'll altho have to take another look around your plathe."

"Do whatever you need to do, Stan. I appreciate all your hard work. It seems so far we are at a dead end, though."

"No, Ed—jutht a fork in the road. But we'll follow every latht lead and look at every latht thpot in every latht corner to find thith thlippery perp…"

Chapter 22

Although I was an admirer of snakes, my confidence went slack when I was asked to treat Bal and Monty—a red-tailed boa constrictor and an albino python. Henri Marcel, an accomplished artist, had adopted them thirteen years ago, shortly after Henri had become a widower. I first met Henri at a pet supply store where I was posting a notice about my services.

"Ah—an an-ee-mal terapeest?" he inquired.

"Yes, that's right. Pardon me for asking, but where are you from? I just love your accent."

"O-rigin-ally, from Mone-trall. Zen, I moved to New York Ceety and now I leeve een Pres-tone Hollow—way up in zee mountains. You mean to say zat I steel have an accent after all of zees time?" I giggled like a little schoolgirl at his flirty silliness. I guessed he was in his late sixties. He had thinning, bright white hair, loads of lovely laugh lines and sparkling hazel eyes. He was quite debonair. "So how's 'bout you—where do you leeve?"

"Well, I must say that my history is not as diverse as yours. I've lived my whole life in this general area, but Ed and I live up in the mountains now, too, not that far from you."

"Well—how za 'bout zat! Do your serveeces eenclude reptiles?"

"I love reptiles! But just what are you referring to exactly?"

"I have two very do-cile snakes—a boa constreector and pyton. Zay are my babies but are getting old and steef, like moi."

"Aw', go on—you're still a youngster," I teased.

"At zee very least, I am steel young at heart."

Henri was most definitely a charmer—hence, the snakes?

"Well, I would love to come visit your snakes. When do you think would be a good time?"

Henri gave me his phone number and address and we set a date.

When I first arrived at his home, the overall aesthetics and serenity of the place flabbergasted me. The house sat on a tiered piece of land that provided a spectacular view of the Catskill Mountains. Between the passion for life that Henri exuded and the sun pouring through the grand windows in the main living area, a warmth enveloped me and I somehow felt at home. Henri took me on a brief tour of the place. When we entered his art studio, I nearly fainted with delight. His works were overwhelmingly emotional and varied. I was in awe, wandering through each of his creations. "Your work is so amazing," I stupidly said, meaning to express so much more.

"I can see zat you are an arteest by zee way you eenspect my work. What me-di-um do you work weeth, my dear Rena?"

His art, his words and his manner had truly touched my core. I had welled up and was embarrassed but I somehow knew he wouldn't care. "Henri—you, your work, your home—I am so bowled over by your passion and grace."

"Ah, Rena! You are so very sweet. I am so very grateful for your love of art and nature. But, my dear, you never deed answer my question, eh?"

"Oh, Henri, I'm such an amateur. I only dabble in oil and watercolors. I've played some with chalk and oil pastels but I'm only able to paint when I have a little free time, which isn't much. I haven't been able to do enough to really develop any personal technique."

"Well, what would you say if Henri helps you out by geeving petit lessons at zee end of each veeseet you have with Bal and Monty—how's zat?"

"That, Henri, would be more than super. Now where are those two 'babies' of yours?"

He then led me to yet another spectacular sunroom area where Bal and Monty were curled side by side sleeping peacefully. Henri lifted the larger Monty and draped him around his shoulders, then pointed with a nod to Bal indicating I should follow suit. "I have to tell you, Henri, I'm a little nervous. My only experience with big guys like these has been watching them from behind glass at the zoo. But I sure do love my little garden snakes..."

Chapter 23

Lydia had taken a much-needed break from the computer and her overwhelmingly confusing research on poisons. She decided that cleaning up the dead debris in my flowerbeds left by winter's wrath would be a fruitful diversion. Many of the spring bulbs were starting to bloom and Lydia thought she would try her best to keep the beds as she knew I would want them. Lydia had traveled back to her own home and family once during the past week. She needed to be near them, not only to know they were safe but also to escape the insanity of my reality. The idea that someone had maliciously murdered me was incomprehensible. Lydia was pruning dead canes from my roses when she looked up to see Blake coming down our long driveway. Lydia ran to him and gave him a solid, lasting hug—neither of them wanting to let go.

"I had to see you, Lydia. I have not been able to sleep very well. I swear Rena is talking to me." Blake fought back his tears and said, "I know it sounds crazy but I truly think she's trying to tell me something. I keep hearing her say the word 'banjo,' but I have no idea what that means. I feel like I'm totally losing it."

"Sweetie, you're not losing it—not any more than the rest of us. I dream about her every night, too, but my dreams are all discombobulated. I'm always frenzied and trying to find her, as if she's a lost child, but I know I'm running out of time. Everywhere I look I see a clock ticking and know if I don't get to her by a certain time, she'll be gone forever."

Now they were both crying and again holding on to one another for dear life.

"Mom and Dad desperately want to come up," Lydia said, "but I think they should wait until we are able to get Rena's body back—don't you?"

"Yeah—there's nothing they can do right now—or later for that matter."

"I told them we're planning to just get the immediate family together for the disposal of her ashes. Then we'll gather the whole family and their friends for one giant group hug later in the day. Does that sound okay with you?"

Blake looked so distraught. "Makes sense to me—I know that's what she would want. You know what I'd like to do, Lydia? I want to go look through Rena's paintings. Maybe there's something there that will tell me more—I don't know. I know that sounds silly but I just feel so helpless."

"I think it's a great idea and probably therapeutic. While you're doing that, I'm going to go through her gardening supplies again to see if she did have any chemicals on hand, though if the CSI team couldn't find anything, I doubt I will. I just can't imagine how these chemicals could have been introduced to her without her being noticeably ill…"

Chapter 24

"Hey, Nick—do you think you could pick me up this mornin' and bring me to work? My back kinda went out on me last night."

"Yeah, yeah—sure, Marvin. What—did noicie get a little frisky on ya—huh?"

"Heh, heh—yeah, sure—she's a wildcat, that one. Those physical therapy broads really got the moves," Marvin boasted and, as he went to hang up the phone, he cringed and cried out in pain.

After Nick assisted Marvin into his truck, he said, "Geez, Louise! You ain't kiddin' 'bout her bein a wildcat an all. *I* wunnit mind gettin' a piece of dat action myself. Whaddya think, Marv—would she go a round wit' me?"

Marvin snickered and said, "Yeah, Nick—you could definitely handle a broad like her. Give her a call—*I* certainly don't give a shit." Marvin grinned just thinking about the scene.

Once at the garage, Nick dialed my number. "Hey, noicie—it's me—Nick."

"This better be good," I growled.

"Ohhh—so's yous is hurtin', too—huh?"

"What the hell do you want, Fagioli?"

"Sheesh—I was just wondrin' if yous wouldn't mind goin' a round wit' me later on—you know, like yous did last night wit my friend, Marvin."

"What—you want me to kick your ass like I did Marvin's—is that what you're saying, Nick?"

"You kissed his ass?"

"**Kicked**, Fagioli—I *kicked* his ass—sent him flying across the room!" Silence on the other end. "Oh—didn't he tell you, Nick?"

"Uh—yeah—heh, heh—he told me. I just wanted ta tease ya 'bout it." CLICK.

"Huh—guess I pissed her off. Hey, Marvin! What's the story here? I just got hung up on by noicie."

"You moron! You really thought she went for me? I was kiddin', Nickie. How the hell long have you known me now…?"

Chapter 25

"So, how long *have* you known Ed Lorence?" Miller Sampson asked the sexagenarian behind the front desk at the free clinic.

"Aw, I've known Eddie now for quite some time. He takes extra good care of me."

Miller was questioning the "boozing" woman Gus Freeman had mentioned on the ride back to the shelter—Elisha Looby. She was one of the poor, older souls Ed had adopted. "Do you think you can you give me a more specific number in terms of weeks, months or years that you've been acquainted?"

Elisha dropped her head and sat in a glazed silence for an awfully long minute—possibly two. Elisha was one of Ed's long-term patients and one he had come to know and love dearly. Miller wasn't sure if she had completely gotten lost somewhere in there and finally cleared his throat in an attempt to gently bring her back to the present. Lifting her head and looking at Miller as if for the first time, she answered his question slowly but with a sure accuracy. "Ed began volunteering for the clinic before he retired. I remember that because I used to constantly tell him that he was going to burn out with working both full-time at the hospital and part-time here at the clinic. He and I hit it off immediately. He's the one who got me off the hooch."

"Really? You don't drink at all anymore?" Miller had doubts.

"No, sir, Mr. Sampson—I don't," Elisha assured. "I realize I'm a little off balance—both on my feet and in my thoughts—so though I may still appear as a drunk—believe you me—I'm as sober as a non-celibate priest reliving a Kodak moment. Ed pulled me out of the toilet—literally and figuratively. He got me into rehab and saw me through it. Now I'm able to work here part-time as a file clerk and volunteer at the shelter where I still live. So to answer your original question, I've known Eddie for five years."

Miller was jotting in his notebook and still trying to hold back a laugh at the non-celibate priest bit. He bit his cheek and proceeded. "Has he ever brought you to his home?"

"Oh, you bet! Eddie and Rena have been incredibly generous. They have treated me like family since day one. I have been so distraught over the recent news of Rena's death." Elisha had what could be best described as ruts in her face rather than wrinkles but, since she had stopped drinking, she had gained a sparkle in her eyes that could light up a room. Now they were suddenly filled with sorrow. Miller was surprised at how articulate she could be for a down-and-out recovering lush.

Miller pondered whether he should ask, but couldn't resist. "How did you become homeless, Elisha? You seem to be a very intelligent woman."

"Well, hon, have you got time?"

"I'm all ears," Miller replied.

Elisha poured them both a cup of coffee and began. "Well, my friend, it all started as a result of my peregrinating family. Yes, sweetie—the carnival. We were quite a zany group and were filled with wanderlust—'afoot and lighthearted' as Walt Whitman said. For an impressionable young girl, it was enchanting—I'd even say mystical. We eventually settled down—for a few years at least—in the small town of Bohemia on Long Island, following in the footsteps of our ancestors who had spent many years on the outskirts of the Bohemian Forest in Austria. I was in my late teens then. My family actually let me attend college for a time to study business management and accounting. I was able to help out with the family business for a long time and we did very well. Before our town was built up, we were even able to keep some of our large, retired cats at home. Our pet tiger, Spot, who died of old age was buried right in the back yard along with the rest of our deceased housecats and dogs. Can you imagine some time in the future when excavators dig up that huge cat skeleton among the smaller ones? I laugh every time I think of it! I would love to see their faces!" Elisha paused a moment to happily reflect and then continued. "Anyway, getting back to the original subject—the carnival world, at times, could be quite prosperous but desperate at others as you might well imagine. We ended up back in Europe where we knew we could draw larger crowds in the ancient towns and villages. I ended up married to a distant cousin—which was acceptable in those days - especially in carny circles. We were a passionate couple until I learned he was just as hot for any other curvy creature that crossed his path. After our bitter divorce, I hit the bottom of a bottle or two every night. I neglected my job and made huge mistakes with the books, which could not even be forgiven by family. Every cent counted back in those days—still does. Anyway, they tossed me out on my ass, told me to straighten up and went on their way. They left me high and well—just high—somewhere in Europe. I've been homeless in all parts of the world, hooking up with dreamers and schemers who got me from place to place. I ended up here over ten years ago. When Eddie came along, he took great interest in me. He seemed to look deeper than most and saw me as a human being. He gave me something that saved my life—a sense of hope and self-respect. I was blown away by his first invitation to his home and his and Rena's overwhelming hospitality. Ever since, we've been great friends."

Miller was looking at Elisha with feelings of both amazement and disbelief but she had definitely touched a nerve. Considering her past history and current circumstances, she displayed a bizarre sort of eloquence. "Do you know of anyone who may have wanted to hurt Rena or Ed?"

"Honestly, Mr. Sampson, no, though out of all the people who have come and gone there is one person who just somehow rubs me the wrong way…"

Chapter 26

After about three weeks with Tweaker, I had finally convinced Tiffany to clean up her apartment so that Tweaker had some actual walking space. I assisted her with organizing all the junk that was strewn about and dumping her wealth of trash. We got to see Tweaker walk across the floor for the first time ever. He became fascinated with the shows she'd have running on TVLand and would dance—crest fully erect, mind you—to their opening theme songs. He was a proud and happy bird now. I discharged him from treatment after five visits, Tiffany squawking with joy. I snidely joked and advised her not to jump up and down as she might knock an eye out. Dumbfounded, she asked, "With what? My clutter is gone."

I simply responded, "Never mind," shaking my head and snickering as I exited.

I had never expected to willingly return to the Duffer household but a week later, while I was shopping at BJ's wholesale club, I came across a video of Robert Blake's old TV series *Baretta*. Chuckling to myself, I thought it would be a perfect gift for Tweaker and Tiffany. As I pulled up to Duffer's mobile abode, I saw a tow truck in the driveway. 'Great—Marvin has another day off,' I thought. I almost kept going but realized I wouldn't be in this part of town again for a while and wasn't about to make another trip for something this trivial. I knocked on the door and waited a few minutes. Just as I was about to turn and leave, I heard muffled screams. The adrenaline shot through me once again like an exploding pincushion. The door was unlocked so I barged in. There was Tweaker dancing in front of the TV, seemingly unruffled by the cries. First, I armed myself with one of Tiffany's fry pans and then followed the sounds. I was quite relieved to see that the floor was still clear of litter so that I could maneuver. I called Tiffany's name out loud and again heard a throaty moan. I could only imagine that Marvin was rendering some horrendous, sadistic form of punishment—he had to be stopped. I burst into the room and there was Tiffany—spread eagle—with Nick Fagioli aboard for the flight.

"*WHOA!* It's da noice! I taut she was done over 'ere, huh? What was you tinkin'?"

I turned partially to avoid the offensive scene and sternly asked, "Are you okay, Tiffany?"

"Oooh, yeah. I'm so sorry you had to see this. You ain't gonna say nothin', will ya?"

"No, I won't. I just thought you were in trouble when I first came in. I stopped by to drop off a present for Tweaker. I'll leave it on the TV." I heard Tiffany utter a "Tanks" but, as I walked out of the place, trying to shake off the jitters, the last words I heard were, "You say a woid to James and yous'll be wishin' ya hadn't…"

Chapter 27

'Rena, how the hell could this ever have happened to us?' Ed thought as he made his was over to see Dom. Ed ached in his weariness and a constant worry as to whether he could have possibly done anything to prevent me from cashing in all my chips so soon. A younger Modigliani was boxing up a couple dozen fancy Italian cookies for a customer when Ed walked in. Asking to speak with the young man's father, Ed was told he could find Dom at the Hope Hill Cemetery. "He goes there every day to have his lunch with my mom. She died recently in an attempted robbery here."

"Yes, I know. Rena had told me all about it—I'm so, so sorry."

"Oh—Madonna-me! You're Rena's husband! No, *I* am the one who's sorry. My dad loved Rena. When he found out she had passed, he bawled like a baby—more so even than he did for my mom—I swear. She was a sweetheart, that Rena. Hey, why don't you go find my dad—I'm sure he'd love it if you joined him."

"Thanks—I think I'll do just that. And I appreciate the kind words about Rena. I'll take a loaf of that warm, Italian bread and some of those hot olives—wouldn't want your Dad to eat alone."

Ed found Dom at Gina's graveside, sitting on a picnic blanket with his lunch sprawled in front of him. He was sipping a glass of red wine.

Ed could see from a short distance that Dom was talking. He made his way toward Dom slowly and hesitated, so as not to interrupt his train of thought. When Dom became quiet, Ed approached him and introduced himself. Dom welled up immediately, patting the blanket in a silent gesture for Ed to join him. Dom poured Ed a chianti and said with a sigh, "Your Rena—she was'a some gal'a. She'a not only made'a little Guy feel good'a but'a made me'a feel human once again'a." Dom proceeded with his reminiscences of how I would meet him at the cemetery for lunch and give Guy his treatment at the same time. He said I had gotten Guy well enough to chase a Frisbee again. I had wanted to discontinue therapy for Guy as I felt he was well enough but Dom begged me to continue on. "Rena felt bad about'a bein' paid for just'a playin' wit'a little Guy, but I insist'a she stay on'a. Why let a good'a ting go, eh?"

Ed and Dom continued to chat for over an hour. Ed was convinced that Dom had nothing to do with my giving up the ghost. Ed had initially been quite shaken to hear Dom describe our treatment sessions at the cemetery though. I had never mentioned it to Ed and I'm not altogether sure why. Ed didn't want to upset Dom any further but suddenly felt the need to ask, "Did the police ever apprehend the guy who killed your wife, Dom?" Dom looked at Ed with surprise and said, "Yes! Didn'a Rena tell'a you? Da guy had'a da nerve'a to come back in'a da store'a. The cops had'a been'a surveillin' da place wit'a hopes he'd'a come back at'a da scene of 'a da crime'a. Rena was atta' da shop—she saw da whole'a ting'a."

Ed was stunned. He felt like he'd been slapped. I guess I had never said a thing about that either. "When did this all take place, Dom?"

"It was'a day right'a before Rena passed'a." Dom made a quick sign of the cross and kissed his pinched-together fingertips.

Ed just didn't get it. He kept thinking, 'Why hadn't Rena been telling me these things? We normally shared everything.' Now he was extremely worried about what else I may not have mentioned.

Ed thanked Dom for sharing his special time at Gina's gravesite and, of course, the chianti. About halfway home Ed decided to turn around and headed for the BCI office instead. He needed to tell someone in person—hopefully Miller—about what he had just learned. He could feel a headache coming on...

Chapter 28

Ralph greeted me on my seventh visit to treat Moose frowning and pallid. "I'm sorry, Rena. I forgot about you coming today. I have a horrible migraine and need to rest. You'll have to come back another time." He had barely opened the door to his apartment and I could see he must have pulled his shades, as it was unusually dark behind him. There was no sign of Moose who was normally right there to usher me in.

"I could work with Moose outside if you'd like and quietly let him back in when we're through. I hate to have him miss a treatment."

"No, Rena—I have to go lie down. Call me tomorrow," and with that, closed and bolted the door.

'Hmm,' I thought, 'very strange.' I was a little miffed about wasting my time and gas, but then I remembered something I had wanted to investigate since my first visit here. I hadn't yet had the opportunity because Ralph had always left during Moose's treatments to visit his mother. I walked out to my car and noted where Ralph had parked. His car was not in the familiar place, which could always be seen from his apartment window. Instead it was around the corner on the opposite side of the building. I looked up at his shade-covered living room window and didn't see him spying out at me. I decided to pull my own car out of the lot entirely and park down the street. That way, I could easily walk back to his car to check for hand controls without him seeing me. To be on the safe side, I decided to throw on my long-billed, black baseball cap and wide, black sunglasses to provide some disguise. I rolled my braid up inside my cap and threw on the old, ratty brown jacket I kept in the car for my days at the animal shelters. The sun was just about to set and as I stepped off the curb to cross the street leading back to the lot, I saw Ralph's car coming right at me. I could also see the setting sun was blinding him, as he was trying to adjust his visor and I knew he didn't see me at all because he was not slowing down. I quickly back-stepped up the curb and turned ninety degrees to walk in the opposite direction of his car. I didn't dare look back until I knew the car was out of sight. Just to be sure it was Ralph's car, I ran to the lot. Sure enough—his car was gone. Then I noticed there was an emergency door being held open by a videotape right in front of where his car had been parked. I hadn't noticed that the door was opened before. I walked to it quickly, grabbed the tape and shoved it under my jacket. As I rushed back to my car, I wondered what the hell *his* hurry had been. He sure didn't waste any time leaving. Maybe there was an emergency with his mother, but I highly doubted it. My suspicions about him were mounting. I had wanted to believe he was sick—he had certainly looked it from the small gap he created when he answered the door—but I should have known…

Chapter 29

Miller rapped on Tiarra Smythe's door using the grotesque gargoyle knocker, which seemed completely out of place on the tiny, baby-blue clapboard cottage. A pentacle hung to the left of the door. Tiarra's résumé was engraved in it, with each point naming one of her special talents—Psychic, Channeler, Tarot Reader, Palmist, Astrologer—and smack in the center it read—Witch. 'Oh, boy,' Miller thought, 'nut case central.' Across the street he noticed a funeral in progress and suddenly felt both angry and sad.

The door flung wide open and Chris asked, "Can I help you?" Miller showed his ID as he introduced himself and asked to speak with Tiarra. Chris advised she was in a session but said she'd be available in about ten minutes if he wanted to hang around that long. Miller said he'd wait and told Chris the crux of his visit. "OH! Tiarra *wants* to talk with you—she *knew* you were coming!"

Miller chuckled to himself, thinking 'Of course she did—there's a full-blown investigation going on—how could she not know?' Miller stood amidst the messy clutter, eyeing as much as he could without being overly conspicuous. Chris, wearing a cropped white t-shirt, mint-green jogging pants and clogs, offered him tea and pranced out of sight to the kitchen. Miller pondered Chris' gender. When Chris reappeared, Miller asked, "And how are you related to Tiarra?" Chris went into his usual marketing spiel and Miller still couldn't tell, deciding to just save his energy for more important matters. After a few more minutes of assessing his surroundings, Miller finished his tea. He was beginning to feel antsy. Just then Tiarra emerged with her client, a middle-aged, well-to-do-looking sort. He was wiping tears from his face with his personally embroidered handkerchief, thanking Tiarra profusely. Again, Miller thought, 'The world is full of 'em.' When the gentleman paid and left, Miller was about to proceed with his questioning, when Tiarra's jaw flopped open and out spouted her psychic findings.

"Rena was a sweet girl, but she did have a few enemies—not because of anything she did but because of something she knew. I didn't sense a foreboding when she was treating our Punzey but I had visions of her being in trouble afterward. I know she was poisoned—that was in all the papers—but it took place slowly over a period of weeks. That's why she was that hideous gray when she died—that dead gray—from the mix of poisons and the effects they had on her blood and nerves. She didn't suffer until the very end—that last lethal dose. She was paralyzed. She couldn't move or speak to ask for help."

Tiarra paused to catch her breath, long enough for Miller to suspiciously ask, "Why didn't you notify anyone of your 'visions'?"

Tiarra looked embarrassed and meekly said, "I've done that in the past and I was way off the mark. I would just scare the hell out of the people who had star billing in my head and then never hear from them again. I've been on an anti-depressant for years, which gives me the most vivid dreams. Some were so real I felt they were true. After being wrong a few times, I didn't want to chance ruining my reputation any more than I already have."

Miller was actually dazzled by her description of my color and literal cause of death—the final paralysis, of which no one else knew but the coroner. A distrust of her was incubating. He reproachfully asked, "Do you have *any* clue as to who may have poisoned Rena?"

Tiarra looked painfully at Miller and said, "I really don't trust myself to say. Like I said before, I have vivid dreams—I could be terribly wrong." She paused in an attempt to avoid saying anything more, but Miller's half-pleading, half-commanding eyes urged her on. "It was someone close to her—I do feel that—and they slept peacefully as she died." Tiarra was now visibly shaken and teary.

Chris suddenly piped up and nervously croaked, "Was it her *husband?*"

"No, no—I don't think it was her husband," Tiarra quickly responded. "I know he was *very* choked up about her death. I also know he holds the key."

Miller found her choice of words interesting as he thought back to the day the deputy sheriff and EMTs arrived at our home and what they had reported about Ed when he answered the door. "Just tell me as much as you can, even if you feel doubtful as to the details. We'll weed through it all and decide what can be used. I give you my word that, in no way, will we do or say anything to harm your reputation." Miller suddenly felt in his gut that Tiarra's display of emotion was filled more with sympathy than remorse. He believed her when she said she hadn't seen me since autumn of the previous year. His incubating suspicion had just hatched and got fried.

"Well," she started, the words coming at a much slower and more thoughtful pace than before, "for some reason, in the background of my visions, there has been music. I really don't know what that means other than there's a possibility that a musical instrument or musician could have been involved—something of that nature. There's also someone—can't decipher male or female—either with a ton of money or no money. I know I'm not being very clear but money is somehow involved—and a key. This is where Ed Lorence comes in. There's definitely a real key that will open the door to explain Rena's death. That's really all I have for you right now." Tiarra all at once looked like she had just run a marathon.

Miller had been taking copious notes and, though he couldn't be sure whether or not Tiarra was a full-blown loon, greatly thanked her for the information. Tiarra readily complied with Miller's request to have a look around, though he had no warrant, which then placed her well toward the bottom of any list of suspects. "If you think of anything else at all, Ms.

Smythe, please call me," handing her his card as he stood to leave.

Tiarra said, "I'll keep trying to see more into this case and restrain from reading about it in the papers. After all, I wouldn't want you to think I'm cheating…"

Chapter 30

I had worked with Butch and Jamie for four weeks, fostering Jamie's abilities to take over the therapy, as Butch's leg became more limber. Butch was now able to walk on the leg—though with a slight hiccup—but no longer seemed to be in pain. Jamie understood that Butch needed to do as much on his own as possible and so I also provided leash training. No more free pocket rides for Butch and plenty more chances for Jamie to get out of the house and experience the world beyond Nick Fagioli.

I had also gently shucked Jamie out of her shell during this time and discovered a real gem. I had been worried for her physical and mental well-being after seeing how Nick had talked to her on that first day. Then after surprising Nick at Tiffany Duffer's—of all places—and catching that threatening, hardball tone in my gut as I walked out the door, I feared for her safety all the more. I began asking her simple, personal questions to get her to loosen up with me, unobtrusive inquiries about her past and family. I offered up the same information to her. After a while, I dove into more of her personal life with Nick—how they met, their courtship, when they got married. Our conversations became deeper and more intimate. Jamie informed that her parents were Sicilian—very old school. Men in her family were treated like royalty and women like peons. Her parents had essentially pre-arranged her courtship with and eventual marriage to Nick, as they were very close friends with the Fagiolis.

"I really didn't mind gettin' fixed up with Nickie. He was so handsome and charmin'-like. We dated exactly six months when he axed for my hand in marriage. I was so thrilled—I ran right out to buy my gown and shoes—there was a big sale goin' on at The Bridal Barn. We got married one month later and started right away tryin' to have kids. Nickie wanted a son so bad—it's all he ever talked about. He was wearin' me out, if ya know what I mean."

"Heh—yeah—I get your drift. So you never got pregnant?"

"No—that's the sad part. I was havin' a lot of bleedin'. They told me I had some 'end-a-meat-roses' or somethin' and could never have kids. Nickie almost went through the roof when I told him. He did alotta screamin' and I just bawled my eyes out. What else could I do?"

"He didn't hit you at all, did he?" I reticently asked.

"Nah—he's never hurt me in that way—only by yellin' and callin' me names. We don't have no more love life to speak of, but I feel in my heart of hearts he still loves me."

"I'm sure he does still love you..."

"Now what da hell is yous two talkin' 'bout here?" It was Nick. He was standing just beyond the kitchen doorway where we couldn't see him after he stealthily came in the back way. Who knows how long he may have been listening, but he didn't sound all too pleased.

"We was just talkin' 'bout how I can't have no babies, Nickie—that's all," Jamie said softly and ashamedly.

"Oh, yeah? Ya sure der was nuttin' else, Miss Noice?" Nick's accusatory ammo was hitting me with sniper precision.

"Why, Nick?" I dared. "What else would possibly have anything to do with what you heard us saying?" Boy, oh, boy—talk about your brass balls.

"Uh—nuttin', I guess." Nick's tone dropped a hair, but the scope of his glare that was still aimed my way would have made anyone want to duck and cover. I wouldn't give him the pleasure of looking away. As he angrily doffed that same Carhartt jacket I remembered from the first visit, another feather fell to the floor. I looked over at Jamie to see if she noticed but she still had her head lowered in atonement, as if she had just gone to confession. Butch hippity-hopped his new gait over to inspect what was now going to be his new chew toy, picking up the feather and dutifully parading back over to show his mommy. Jamie retrieved it from his teeth and said, "Well, wouldya look at this—a featha. Where ya supposin' it came from?"

I tossed Nick an abrupt sneer but to save Jamie's already hurt feelings said, "Oh, that must have fallen from my bag. In my travels, I see all sorts of *creatures*," emphasizing the last word as I glanced back at Nick. He had actually lost his composure and blushed, disbelieving the fact that I covered for him.

"Doesn't Marvin's girlfriend have a bird, Nickie?" Jamie's words sprung at him so fast he ducked.

Wanting to see him cower just a little longer, I innocently asked, "Marvin's girlfriend?"

Nick stammered, "Uh, yeah—her name is—uh—Tiffany—uh, yeah—I tink she does have a boid, James." Now his face was crimson and his message to me reflected in those all-black eyes was venomous.

"Oh, yes," I glibly acknowledged. "That's right—Tiffany Duffer—she does have a cockatoo that I treated a few weeks ago. Guess I didn't realize she was Marvin's girlfriend though, now that I think of it, she did mention him once."

"So you ain't goin' over to treat the bird no more?" Jamie guardedly asked.

"No, but the feather was probably still stuck in my bag—pretty, isn't it?"

The dead air was intense as we all stared at the feather. I had definitely had about enough of all this bullshit, so I made a hasty decision. "Well, listen, you two. I think that Butchie has made great progress. Now that Jamie has mastered the leash training and is comfortable helping him with his exercises, this will be my last visit."

"Good call," Nick spat.

Jamie welled up and said, "Ya really was great in helpin' Butchie—and me. I'll sure miss ya. Wouldya mind if I took a snapshot of ya wit' Butchie so I'll have somethin' to rememba ya by?"...

85

Chapter 31

It had already been two weeks since I bit the big one. Lydia and Blake were reminiscing with Ed as they flipped through old photo albums. Ed was telling them how he had gotten a call from Miller the day before. "You know, he's actually consulting a psychic on the case who just happens to be one of Rena's old clients. He's coming over later so we can brainstorm, if you guys want to hang around for that. Miller told me that this woman thinks I have a key—a real key—which will unlock the truth in this case. She sounds like a crackpot to me."

Lydia stared at the group photo from the last family get-together. Her eyes rose to meet Ed's with a quizzical look and she asked, "What if—just what if—this supposed psychic had something to do with Rena's death? She could throw Miller completely off track."

"Miller checked her out and said he's pretty much eliminated her as a suspect," Ed reported. "I've got to trust the guy. He knows his stuff."

Blake said, "Lydia, we can certainly tell Miller of any doubts we have but I really think he should follow every possible lead no matter how silly or crazy it may sound at the time. I totally believe in psychic abilities—you know that—but I also realize there are a lot of imposters out there. Let's just see what she has to say and go from there."

Ed and Lydia raised an eyebrow at Blake, but simultaneously said, "You're right." They all looked at one another and laughed. "You owe me a Coke," they both said again in stereo. "Cut it out!" again in sync.

"Okay, you two—knock it off—I'm creeping out here!" Blake said with a semi-smirk and a slight chill up his spine.

Lydia said, "That is pretty eerie—I know what you mean. Rena and I used to say the same things together constantly—or one of us would think it and the other one would say it. At times, we would buy the same exact piece of clothing even though we were shopping separately."

Ed added, "Not only did Rena and I say the same things at the same time, but we used to *dream* the same dream on the *same* night!"

Lydia and Blake screamed together. "Me, too!"

"Okay, this is getting way too weird for me," Ed said as he raised both hands in a signal to stop. "I do think, though, that Rena was psychic somehow in her own little way even though I don't believe in that kind of nonsense—at least I thought I didn't. I just wish Miller would get here so we could get some more insight," Ed anxiously said. He had begun pacing as he always did when he felt uneasy. The phone rang and Ed dashed for it. "Hello? Yes, Miller. Oh? Well, sure, I guess. I don't see why not. That should prove quite interesting actually. Okay, see you in a bit."

"Well?" Lydia asked.

"Miller is going to pick up psychic lady and bring her here today," Ed advised.

"That's great!" Blake said. "She may be able to sense a lot more being here in Rena's home surroundings."

Ed had gone back into his pacing mode but had upped the speed a notch. Lydia squeezed her lips together in an attempt not to say anything and slowly shook her head as she followed Ed with her eyes. Finally she said, "Ed, honey. Maybe you should try to relax a little—have a drink or something. You're wearing yourself thin—not to mention the carpet..."

Chapter 32

"Come in but please remove your shoes. We just had wall-to-wall installed last week."

That was my welcome the first time I visited the home of Selma and Louis Derrow. I immediately noted the fact that they were both still wearing *their* shoes. They were an elderly couple, she in her seventh and he in his eighth decade. They seemed to be quite well off—at least according to the airs they put on—but their house was relatively modest. They had called me concerning their eight-year-old poodle, Bernard. Apparently he had been very sluggish lately and Selma said their vet recommended my services.

"So what's been bothering Bernard, Mrs. Derrow?"

"Oh, please, call me Selma, won't you?"

"You can call me Mr. Derrow," Louis Derrow piped in, laughing heartily as he said it—but somehow I knew he fully meant it. He reminded me of a WC Fields type—a real curmudgeon—minus his humor.

"Oh, Louis—stop it," Selma politely quipped, with a limp wave of her hand. "Bernard has not been right lately and that's why the vet is keeping him for observation for a few days. He's had a constant problem with clogged anal glands and if he's not sliding his derriere across the floor, he's sulking. He has simply lost his will."

I was gasping yet giggling to myself, picturing (in smell-a-vision) the horrendous task of untapping those glands but enjoying the visual of Bernard wiping his plugged-up ass all over their new, cream-colored carpeting. "Oh, my," I proclaimed, however insincerely. "I hope the vet didn't mislead you. I don't take care of stopped-up anal glands."

"Oh, no, my dear—not to worry. The vet is taking care of that problem. But he does need some added attention as far as exercise goes. I will gladly pay you extra if you could take the time to visit three times a week to walk and exercise him."

"Oh, I see. Well *that* I can definitely do. It's a deal." And with a ladylike handshake, Selma and I settled on a price and scheduled my first three visits.

From the living room, I could hear Louis grumbling something about his money being pissed away on a dog walker and then he yelled in bully-like fashion, "*Selma*! It's cocktail time—where's my Scotch?"...

Chapter 33

Ed had settled down some after having a mid-day Bloody Mary. Blake and Lydia had continued looking at photos and tearfully reliving happy times. Ed caught movement out of the corner of his eye and announced the arrival of Miller's vehicle in the driveway. All three watched from the windows as Miller walked around to the passenger side of his car to hoist this bulky woman out of her seat.

"Holy shit," Ed muttered. "Scary."

"Nice coif," Lydia threw in.

"Now, now, you two," Blake said, "behave."

Ed opened the door and invited them in, making the round of introductions. Tiarra immediately started looking all around the room like she was following a bubble in flight. "She's here. She is so much here," she spookily vowed.

Ed, Lydia, Blake and Miller all looked back and forth at one another in frightful disbelief. Lydia asked, "What do you mean exactly by 'she's here'? Do you see her—hear her—what?"

"I feel her presence—it's very strong," Tiarra said. "She's telling me she's never left and won't until we find who killed her."

"Wow," Blake said as his eyes misted. "Poor Rena. I'm glad you're here, Tiarra. I have something I want to tell you. I haven't told anyone yet, but I guess this is the right time."

Ed busied himself in making sure everyone had a seat. They all decided to share something that day no matter how slight or ridiculous they felt about it. Ed figured that none of it could hurt and it would certainly, at the very least, be palliative.

Blake proceeded with telling them his story about the music he'd been hearing every night right around 3 a.m. "It's so haunting and soulful, like she's trying to relate her sad tale."

"She died around 3 a.m.," Tiarra said, "and I told you there was music involved," she added as she directed her look toward Miller. Miller noticed Tiarra's self-confidence was building.

Blake continued, "I've also dreamed—at least I think it's a dream—that Rena is alerting me to a banjo. The music I'm hearing though is not the sound of a banjo. The only banjo I can think of is the one that was stored in the attic of the house where we grew up. What ever happened to that banjo, Lydia?"

Tiarra raised her eyebrows again at Miller.

"I have no idea. I had actually asked Mom and Dad the other day after you had mentioned your dream to me the first time, but they don't remember. They thought one of us had taken it."

Ed said, "Rena never had a banjo. I do remember her mentioning the one you had at your house on Younglove Avenue. I think at one time she wondered what had happened to it, too."

"Well, anyway, the only other thing I can think of at the moment is that, when I was looking through Rena's paintings, she had a series of them with titles such as 'Gateway to My Soul,' 'Open Window to My Soul' and so on. There were five of them depicting doorways, gateways, windows—you get the point—that were painted over an eye, as if you were looking through the opening into her eye—into her soul. In every one of them there was a key. The reason the key grabbed my attention was that it was depicted as a teardrop falling from the eye—very conspicuous, yet hidden—in a sense an invitation to enter and find the true meaning of what made Rena tick."

"I *told* you there was a key," Tiarra said in a self-congratulatory way, not even looking toward Miller this time. "Where is this painting? I'd like to take a look at it."

Blake jumped up from his chair and said, "I'll get it. It's on her French easel…"

Chapter 34

Henri and I loved to exchange slithery snake tales at every visit. His, of course, all involved Bal's and Monty's shenanigans, especially when they were younger and more active. Henri's best story was that once when he and his wife were on a flight to the Marquesas Islands, they had snuck their babies on board in a carry-on. Monty escaped the bag somewhere over the Pacific while Henri and his wife napped. Before long total mayhem ensued. "Zey acted as eef Monty was hi-zhacking zee plane, for Christ's sake," Henri crowed. He went on to say they had to pay a hefty fine, keep the babies in quarantine and put them in cargo for the return flight.

My favorite story wasn't quite on par with his but I shared it anyway. I had saved a baby garter from sure death when canoeists were about to hack it to pieces with their paddles. I had quickly snatched it out of the canoe, never pausing to hold it correctly behind the head. Sure enough, it swung around and sunk its teeny teeth into my wrist. "Nice gratitude, you little shit," I scolded and then walked it to the edge of the woods for release, far enough from the brave boatmen.

It was a silly tale but Henri belly-laughed at my enthusiastic interpretation. He spontaneously and surprisingly crossed the room to me and hugged me tightly. He stepped back and gazed into my eyes, uncomfortably long enough for me to look away. Noticing I was disconcerted, he abruptly removed his hands, returned to his seat, and resumed chuckling from the story as if nothing else had happened in between. I had to convince myself that I had imagined any look of infatuation in his eyes or feel of wanting in the length of his embrace. I had been grateful to Henri for giving me painting lessons over the past few weeks and now had to dismiss the thoughts of his close stance behind me as anything other than his interest in art.

Henri seemed to be quite impressed with the comfort in my handling of Bal and Monty over the course of the past month. However, Bal and Monty—though they had their good days—did not seem to be getting much better. They were having digestive problems and the vet said it was only a matter of time. How right he was. At the beginning of my fifth week Monty died and by the end of the week Bal joined him.

"Zey were always a team—never apart," was all Henri could say. We both shed a few tears and then Henri, holding my face and looking at me sweetly, said, "Rena, dear Rena. I so enjoyed your veesits and hope we will remain friends. Zere ees one ting I would like to do for you as a bonus for your time and caring. I would like to buy you a professional French easel."

I looked at Henri disbelievingly, shaking my head "no," but before I could verbally refuse, he said, "I inseest."

So off we went to what had become my favorite art store, thanks to Henri. It was around the Christmas holiday season and the store was jam-packed with shoppers. We wanted to look at an easel that had been set up on an overhead shelf but there were no clerks in sight to give us a hand. I pulled a drafting table close and climbed up to reach the easel. Suddenly I heard a snap and before I had a chance to look down I was sitting on top of a heap. The legs of the table were broken in a freak-of-nature position, like when someone jumps from a building and hits the pavement, their joints extended in places they normally only flex. To top it off, the easel came down with me—damaging other easels on the way—and ended up in many more pieces than intended. A few of the customers gawked but no one said a word, not even to ask if I was okay. None of the store employees came to investigate the calamity. Red-faced and hot-flashing, I stood up slowly, making sure all of my body parts still worked. I looked at the easel and then at Henri and said, "Well? What do you think?"

He shook his head slowly and replied as seriously as he could, "Nah—eet's not quite what I had een mind."

With that, we calmly browsed arm in arm a little longer and then walked out of the store. When we were about halfway to Henri's car in the lot, we started to run. Looking at one another wide-eyed in the car, we burst into laughter. As we settled into satisfied, endorphin-released sighs, Henri unexpectedly dove across the front-seat arm rest and kissed me, holding the sides of my head with the palms of his hands to keep a tight seal. I squeaked my disapproval but he didn't let up as quickly as I hoped. I squeaked again, only grateful for the close-mouthed technique. When he at long last let go, I saw his instant regret. "Henri! What are you thinking?"

"Oh, Rena—I am such an old fool. Pleeze forgeeve me. You have been such a breath of fresh air een my oth-air-wise stale exeestance."

I actually felt sorry for him and told him I'd forgive him if he promised never to mention it to me again or to anyone else—ever. He looked both relieved and hurt. We were quiet for a good part of the ride home until I started replaying the art store debacle in my head. I burst out laughing again and was uncontrollable for a short time, Henri glancing over periodically with only a quiet smile. Once back at his place, I felt exhausted from the adrenaline rush, the sudden kiss and the hilarity of it all. Henri said he had a much better idea than buying me a new easel, adding that neither one of us would be able to show our faces in that store for quite some time to come. He decided he had too many easels taking up space in his studio anyway and could afford to give one up to his "forgeeving and forever friend." "Afterall, I can only work on tree or four paintings at one time," he jested, "and I no long-air paint en plein air." So he retired one of his folding, wooden French easels and passed it on to me, saying, "I can't tank you enough for ev-air-e-ting. Don't be a strange-air, Rena, because of what happened tonight." I raised a finger to my lips to indicate keeping our secret under wraps and walked out the door, easel in tow. "Keep painting, Rena, and keep me abreast of tings…"

Chapter 35

Miller had read my chart on Tweaker and Tiffany Duffer. He arrived at the mobile home park and knocked on Duffer's door with *great* anticipation. Though he knew what to expect, he still stood there bug-eyed and momentarily speechless, astonished that any woman these days would open their door to a complete stranger—topless, to boot.. He looked her straight in the eye and identified himself and his purpose for being there.

"Ooh, sure—come right in. My friend, Tiarra, told me you'd probably want to ask me some questions."

"Did she tell you much about the case?" Miller probed.

"Ooh, no—as a matter of fact, she said she couldn't discuss nothin' with me. We just feel so bad for Rena. Who do you think coulda done it?"

Miller likened her voice to fingernails on a blackboard. He involuntarily shivered. Then spotting a movement in his peripheral vision before stepping inside, he turned quickly, catching one of the neighbors peering through the window blinds. "You're being spied on, you know," Miller told her.

"Yeah, I know. My neighbors are always eyeballin' me. I don't know why they all just don't mind their own beeswax."

"Well," Miller said as sternly as possible, "most women don't go around answering their doors half naked. Do you have any idea how often sexual assaults are perpetrated by someone known to the victim? Aren't you at all concerned for your safety?"

"Ooh, my—stop it! You're scarin' the hell outta me."

"Well, maybe you should be scared and a little more cautious before opening your door next time. Going topless inside your home is one thing but when you open the door to the world that way, you're inviting trouble."

"I guess you're probably right, but now that we're inside, it's okay, right?"

Miller frowned, shaking his head in disbelief. "Ms. Duffer—you don't know me from Adam. What makes you so trusting?"

"Well, um, you said that an attack would come from someone I know and you're right—I don't know you from Adam whoever."

Miller dropped his head and closed his eyes for a second. "Ms. Duffer, please go put something on while I'm here and promise me you'll cover up from now on when you answer your door."

"Ooh, okay, Mr. Sampson. If you say so." Tiffany bounced off into her bedroom.

Miller stepped into the small living room. Tweaker was standing in front of the TV, his eyes glued to a Robert Blake movie. Tiffany came out of her bedroom a minute later—wearing a leopard-print push-up bra.

Miller was about to go into another spiel but decided he'd just be wasting precious breath. 'She's more dense than the fog I've seen on I-81 in PA,' he thought. 'She deserves whatever she gets.' He then mentally slapped himself for thinking that way.

"So, what is it you'd like to know, Mr. S.?"

"Well, what can you tell me about your visits with Rena?"

"Ooh, she was a great gal. She helped me figure out why Tweaker couldn't walk. Then she helped me get my place all picked up and now he's just fine. She gave us that video he's watchin' now."

"Yes, that's great, but was there anything unusual that ever happened here during one of her visits? For instance, did you ever argue or did she ever confide in you about anything you might have thought strange?" After those words had escaped, Miller thought it a joke considering the source.

"Ooh, well, nothin' that happened when she was treatin' Tweaker. But there is somethin' I probably should tell ya but, no, I better not. I'll be in too much hot water. No—I can't."

"You know, Ms. Duffer, if you withhold information that could help us in this case, you could be charged with a crime and sent to jail. We might even find that you were an accomplice in the murder."

"Ooh, God! I can't go to jail! What would happen to Tweaker?" Her pitch was now shooting electrical jolts from Miller's spinal cord to his fingertips. Although he couldn't imagine that what she had to say could be of any significance to the case, he prodded her on. Tiffany went on to describe to Miller the day I caught her in bed with Nick Fagioli. She remembered and recited Nick's last words exactly. "You say a word to James and you'll be wishin' you hadn't." She added, "I was so embarrassed that day but scared too 'cause I had never heard Nickie talk that way. I was even more ascared of what Marvie would do if he was to find out."

"Marvie? James? Who are they?" Miller asked.

"Ooh, Marvie is my boyfriend—Marvin Wormer? He runs Marvin's Auto shop down on Columbia and Remsen Streets. He'd just kill me if he knew. He'd kill Nickie, too—Nickie works for Marvin. And James—Jamie—is Nickie's wife.

"Has either of them been violent with you in the past?"

"Ooh, no—I don't even know Jamie." Miller winced. "But Marvin just might get rough if he finds out *that* little tidbit."

Miller asked a few more questions about Nick and told Tiffany he'd have to question both Nick and Jamie since they had been my clients, too. He assured her he'd question them separately. As a final thought, Miller asked, "Did Marvin and Rena ever meet?"

"Ooh, no. I woulda known if they had. You ain't gonna question Marvin, too, are ya?"

"I may need to speak to him about Nick but I won't mention anything about our conversation today. And thank you for all of the personal information. You've been quite helpful." Miller looked over at Tweaker, who was now dancing to the closing credits. "Looks like he enjoyed the movie…"

Chapter 36

I watched the videotape I had freed from the propped-open exit door of Ralph's building after Ed had gone to bed that night. Initially it seemed to be a bunch of nonsense. Ralph was videotaping people's butts as he sat in line at a CVS pharmacy and then the focus went to the cashier's breasts. A woman's voice in the background kept telling him to stop. His snickering could be heard and he just kept filming. The clerk's name was Sandy—'So that's Sandy,' I thought. He did scan up to her face a couple of times and she seemed to be quite embarrassed. The unknown woman's voice in the background kept chastising Ralph and seemed vaguely familiar. I assumed it was one of Ralph's aides. Next, the tape cut to Ralph's bedroom. One of his aides was cleaning up and changing the sheets on his bed. She certainly didn't seem to know she was being filmed because, at one point, she peeked inside the bathroom and looked over her shoulder as if to make sure she wasn't being watched. The scene suddenly switched to a short take of Ralph in bed with a woman. I couldn't tell if the woman was Sandy from the store or not, but I could certainly determine that Ralph was not paralyzed by any stretch of the imagination. It was difficult to tell whether this woman knew of the filming but I was beginning to think she probably hadn't—dirty bastard. After only a few seconds the tape ended. Now I wondered if he had been filming me in there during my treatment sessions with Moose. My stomach flipped at the thought of this violation. I now knew for my next visit that I'd have to hone my observation skills and do some further investigating. He was definitely worthy of a *CSI* plot and, although this was all so disturbing, I also found it to be exhilarating.

Ralph invited me in and apologized for canceling our last session. "I really am sorry, Rena. I hated to have Moose miss out but I just had to lie down that day and not be disturbed. Those migraines are more immobilizing to me than my paralysis."

I was surprisingly relieved to know he was still lying to me, which meant he really hadn't seen me that day as he sped down the street. Moose came out of the bedroom in the middle of a big stretch, vocalized a yawn and a garbled doggie welcome. He then pranced happily, half-skipping, over to greet me.

"He really missed you last time," Ralph said. "You know I can really see he's doing much better."

"Yes, I think so, too." I hesitated and then said, "Are you going to your mom's today? I was just wondering because I thought I'd take Moose out for a walk before we do his usual treatment and wanted to make sure you gave me the key."

"Oh, sure—no problem."

Rats—he never answered my question but then handed me the key so I assumed he was going. I harnessed up old Moose and led him out the door. I figured I'd make it a short walk since it was our first time out. Plus I wanted enough time to nose around and get the treatment done without throwing off my schedule. Moose and I were two blocks down the road when Ralph passed us tooting and waving. I walked slowly another two blocks and then headed back. Moose really seemed to enjoy his first outing with me—so many smells, so little time. Before we went back to the apartment I thought I'd check out the stairway on the side of the building where Ralph had parked that day. I pushed the second-floor door open and an alarm sounded. 'Damn it!' I quickly took a peek down the stairwell to the outside door and saw there was no elevator access—what a slimeball. As I turned to leave, an elderly man was blocking the way, hands on hips, bushy eyebrows raised questioningly. "And whattya' think you're doing, young lady?"

"I'm so sorry. I wanted to see if Moose here could handle a flight of stairs. I didn't know an alarm would go off," I answered inanely, despite the very visible "Emergency Door Only—Alarm" sign staring me in the face. "How do you turn this thing off?"

The man led me to a door across the hall marked "STORAGE" and opened it with his key. First, he flipped on a light and then the alarm switch to the "off" position. "The only time this switch is turned off is when something like this happens or when it's more convenient for someone to use that side door, which is very rare. Most of the people here need the elevator," he advised. I looked around the room and saw there were several enclosed storage units with assigned apartment numbers, Ralph's being the furthest away on the right. "Once you switch the alarm off, you can use that door all you want. Just remember to switch it back on—got it?"

"Got it—thanks for the info. That really scared the shit out of me." We both stepped back out in the hall and the door closed behind us. The man smiled, shook his head and started back to his own apartment. I turned to bring Moose home when it occurred to me that one of the keys Ralph gave me might actually get me into that storage unit. I casually looked behind me to be sure there was no one in sight and u-turned with Moose at my heels. The apartment key opened the outside door of the storage room. Now I just hoped I could open the unit itself. Jackpot! I took another quick look over my shoulder. Thankfully the door to the unit didn't squeak. I could see a string hanging from the ceiling and pulled it. The unit was illuminated and at the far end there it stood—plain as day—a camera mounted on a tripod, the red 'RECORD' light flashing. And speaking of flashing, the sweat had started to drip more and more with each paranoid second that crept by. I was frozen for only a moment and then tiptoed up to the viewfinder. No doubt about it—there it was—Ralph's bedroom through a wide-angle lens. I shuddered—no pun intended. I turned to hightail it when the realization that there seemed to be *hundreds* of videotapes on the shelves stopped me cold. I decided I'd better get the hell out of there, making sure the unit was dark, locked, the alarm on and the main light off. As I snuck back out into the hall and turned the corner, I heard the elevator doors being yanked open. It was Ralph's nurse, Michelle, with whom I had previously enjoyed working. "Hey! Fancy meeting you here," I said in an attempt to sound casual.

Michelle looked at me oddly and said, "Are you okay? You're so flushed."

"Oh, I just got back from a long walk with Moose. Plus, menopause is wreaking havoc." It sounded as if I was reading from a script. I was playing ping-pong with the thought as to whether or not I should tell all. I figured I'd better hold off until I could think more clearly. "I hate to tell you this, Michelle, but Ralph's not home. He *says* he's visiting his mother."

"That son of a bitch! That's twice in a row now I've wasted this trip." Michelle never minced words.

"Why the last time—the migraine?"

"Yeah—migraine, my ass. That guy is the biggest phony around."

"So if the agency knows he's a fake, why does he keep getting services?"

Michelle was just as disgusted as I was but, in defense of the agency, said, "We know he has mental problems that need to be addressed but he refuses a mental health consult. We can't just pull all services just because he refuses the one he really needs. Knowing that he's 'sick' and pulling out would be negligent but, believe me, I wish we could ditch him."

"Well if you want an outside opinion, I think the onus is on the guy's doctor, not you. Your time could be so much better spent elsewhere. I can't stand how he's bilking the system. I, on the other hand, have to stick it out only because my buddy, Moose here, needs me.

Michelle nodded and shrugged. "Believe me, I agree with you wholeheartedly, but I've been given my orders…"

Chapter 37

"Well, Nickie told me not to say nothin' but I won't lie to ya. He was pretty upset with me on Rena's last day here. He didn't like the fact that I was tellin' Rena about our personal business but I really trusted her." Miller was almost done with his interview with Jamie Fagioli. "She's the only person I felt I could talk to about it. Nickie seemed to be awful mad at her when he first came in but right after she left he screamed at me pretty good."

"And you're being honest with me that Nick has never abused you physically—never even pushed you?"

"No—I mean, yes—I'm positive. With Nickie, it's always just yellin'—that's all. He's broken furniture and dishes and stuff but he's never hurt me—not in that way."

Miller thanked her for the information and said he'd need to go talk to Nick at work. "Don't worry, Mrs. Fagioli. I won't say anything to get you into trouble." Fifteen minutes later, Miller walked up to the front desk at Marvin's Automotive, the smells of smoke and engine lubricants infiltrating his nostrils. A woman appearing to be in her sixties was sitting at the reception area, crooking a phone between her ear and shoulder as she wrote up an order. A cigarette, holding on desperately to a one-inch ash, bobbled in her cracked lips as she croaked out the order in confirmation. Enveloped in her own second-hand smoke, she looked up at Miller through one squinted, red eye and held up a crooked index finger indicating she'd be with him in a minute. As she hung up, she took a final, long drag off her cigarette. The accrued ash fell, bursting like shattered glass on the desk. She pursed her lips and sent them flying to the floor with a bellow of smoke, followed by a hacking cough. When she finally looked back up to focus on Miller, he saw she had a plastic valve surgically inserted in her throat and there was smoke seeping out of it. He couldn't help but stare.

"Yeah—what can I do for you? And whaddya think you're lookin' at?"

"Oh, sorry—it's just—well, haven't you ever considered trying the patch?" Miller said with his usual concern and equal disgust for ignorance.

"Eh—what the hell—I'm gonna die anyway. I'd probably roll the patch up and smoke that, too. Might as well just enjoy myself. Now do ya want your car fixed or what?"

Miller said he wanted to see Nick Fagioli. The woman shook her head and obligingly wheezed her way to the service garage. A minute later Nick sauntered into the waiting area wiping his hands on an already grease-soaked rag. "Uh, yeah—I'm Nick. Who are you?"

"I'm Miller Sampson from BCI. I'm investigating the death of Rena Lorence. I'd like to ask a f—"

Before Miller could finish his sentence, Nick seethed, "I'll kill that James—well, not kill her—I mean—she betta not be tellin' any of her stories."

"Mr. Fagioli, what are you talking about?"

"Well—uh—I just mean dat my James—my wife, Jamie, dat is—she's not da brightest candle on da cake—or whateva. I just don't know what she may have told ya. She makes tings up, ya know—just ta get some attention—yeah—dat's it."

"What makes you think I spoke with your wife?" Miller slyly posed.

"Uh—I dunno. I was just assumin'."

"Actually, Mr. Fagioli, I only wanted to speak with you—and in private, please." Miller pointed to the door with his eyes to urge Nick to step outside away from the ears of "Dead Woman Walking." Nick obliged and led Miller to the side of the brick building. Miller started with "I spoke with Tiffany Duffer, however. She told me of the surprise visit Rena paid on her and how you just happened to be there. She said you threatened Rena as she left. Is that true?"

"Oh, great. Now dere's anudda example of one dealer short of a card—or sometin' like dat."

Miller looked at Nick with contempt and said, "Funny how you're so attracted to that type—huh, Nick? I see quite a pattern there. Well? What do you have to say?"

Nick, now completely flustered and pacing wildly like a fenced guard dog in the small space Miller allowed between himself and the building, finally sputtered, "So what is it ya wanna know?"

"Did you threaten Rena Lorence as she left Ms. Duffer's that day or not?"

"Nah—I mean I just dinnit want her sayin' nuttin' ta James. I mean somethin' like dat could really hoit her feelin's."

"Aw, gee, Nick. I didn't realize you were such a sensitive guy. I'm touched. Do you recall having any contact with Rena after that day? You know—to follow up on that threat?"

"Nah. She had finished up wit Tiffie and her boid by dat time."

"Didn't you ever see her at your house? Didn't she treat your dog?"

"Oh—uh—right—yeah, yeah. I saw her da day she finished up wit Butchie. She did a great job, dat Rena."

"Did you have any words with her that last day? Any conflict of any kind?"

"Uh—yeah—I had woids. I told her she done a great job—dat's it— no conflict." Nick was having trouble looking Miller straight in the eye.

"Okay then, Nick. If I think of anything else, I'll be dropping by again. I just hope you're telling me all you know." Nick started to re-enter the shop when Miller said, "Oh, yeah—by the way—is Marvin around?"

Nick suddenly looked nauseous, hesitated but eventually stammered, "Uh, uh—yeah. He's in da back—I'll get 'im." Nick threw back a worried glance at Miller but didn't dare open his mouth. A few minutes later, Marvin's skeletal shadow barely sketched the pavement as it sidled

Miller's and Miller was stunned by his nervous demeanor. Miller simply glared at him with the hope of intimidating an eruption of useful information. Instead, Marvin just stared at Miller's shoes in a kyphotic posture. He finally looked up at Miller and grunted, "Yeah?"

"Do you recognize this woman?" Miller asked, as he held a picture of my mug in front of Marvin's face.

"Yeah—I know her. She came to my place one time—uh—to treat my fish," Marvin chortled. "I think she really just wanted to see me," he added smugly.

The fact that Marvin *did* know me took Miller by surprise and he detested his undeserved arrogance. Miller unexpectedly grabbed Marvin by the front of his unctuous shirt and said, "Cut the shit with me, you boney drop of stinking scum! This woman was murdered and if you don't wise up, you're going to become our number-one suspect in this case. Do you have any idea what they do to pathetic, skinny-assed creeps like you in prison these days?"

Marvin's non-existent deodorant was now sorely needed. His sweat—and now possibly other bodily fluids—stained more areas of his automotive-garage garb than one would like to imagine. "Listen, Mr. Sampson! I didn't do anything to that girl. She was a frigid bitch, but I didn't kill her! She totally dissed me, man. She's the one who should be arrested! She assaulted *ME* that night!"

Miller softly smiled and thought, 'Good for you, Rena.' Now, in a frightening calm, Miller's voice was velvet. "She's dead, Marvin. She's dead because she was murdered. Should we arrest her for getting herself murdered, Marvin? Or do you think we should continue with our search for the perp?"

Marvin almost surely peed his pants at this point. It was hard to tell but so much fun watching him squirm. Wormer the Squirmer—how apropos.

Miller dragged Marvin's sorry ass to the precinct for further interrogation about his relationships with Tiffany, Nick, Jamie and me. He really didn't believe Marvin was a viable suspect but he was certainly a slug. Miller wanted to pour more salt on his wounds, watch him writhe and dissolve to the slime he really was. Hearing Marvin blather about his pitiful and suffering existence was like music to his ears…

Chapter 38

"Lulu" and "Yosef" were llamas owned by Franklin and MaryLou McGillacuddy. During my first visit, at least an hour of my time was spent learning more than I really needed to know about the McGillacuddys. They were both in their seventies. Franklin was a retired criminal court judge from the Big Apple and MaryLou had been a US Postal Service employee. She retired with him six years ago as they felt they were ready to begin a new chapter in their lives. They stayed in New York City for four years after retirement but the big-city life was getting too crazy for them. So they decided to settle down in this pastoral place and start a farm. Franklin was hopeful that MaryLou's recently acquired "quirks" might lessen once they moved. He went on to explain how she had always been a little odd for most people's standards but that was part of her charm and why he fell in love with her. But Franklin wasn't sure anymore if she was just eccentric or if the diagnosis could be something more serious. "So why exactly do you need my services?" I asked, trying not to sound impatient. Franklin then went on to explain that he called me because Lulu wasn't responding to his accordion playing lately. "I'm sorry—your accordion?" I thought I had heard it all.

"Yes, you see, I play for them and they come running to me, knowing I'll give them a treat. Then, as I play, they hum and cluck and roll in the dirt."

"Hum and cluck?" I dared ask.

"Yes and sometimes orgle. But Lulu stopped coming to me and she keeps sounding her alarm."

I now wondered just whom the eccentric one was, though I hadn't met his wife yet. It was only 10 a.m.—much too early for something like this—but now I was riddled with curiosity, not only about the missus, but the case of the tone-deaf llama. Or maybe I'd discover that Franklin was the one with the tin ear. Guess I'd soon find out. Franklin led me to the small two-stall pole barn. Sitting on a low stool next to Yosef was a woman wearing a lovely long, lace-trimmed, blue velour evening dress and a pair of mud boots. She was holding a bucket in one hand and a cosmopolitan drink in the other. She looked at Franklin impatiently and said, "They're all dried up! No milk today!" And, with that, stood and walked straight to me, her poise far superior to any I'd ever seen. And, even more remarkably, she hadn't spilled a drop of that cosmo.

"Hello, dear. I am Lady Buggé. Would you care to join me in a cocktail?" She raised her glass and petitely sipped—pinky in the air, natch.

I looked at Franklin questioningly and he apologetically said, "Rena, this is my wife, MaryLou. MaryLou, this is Rena. Rena's going to try to help Lulu get better."

"Well, I sure the hell hope so! We won't ever have any milk at this rate." She then downed the rest of her drink and haughtily sashayed away toward the house.

"I'm sorry," Franklin said. "Maybe I didn't give you enough warning. Like I said, she's a bit eccentric."

I realized I was standing there with my mouth agape and quickly slammed my lips shut. 'Eccentric?' I thought. 'Let's try cuckoo, bananas—out of her freakin' mind!' I cleared my throat and opinions, saying, "No need to apologize, Franklin. She seems perfectly harmless. Just out of curiosity, what did she say her name was again?"

"Well, since we've lived out here, she thinks she's royalty and came up with this name—'Lady Buggé.' I have no idea where she got that one. She also thinks the llamas are cows, in case you didn't notice. Luckily, Lulu and Yosef are very well trained and docile. I don't know what to tell you—maybe it's something in the water," Franklin said with a sad smile.

My guess was that it was more likely what was in that huge martini glass she just emptied...

Chapter 39

Ed was invited to the coroner's office for a more in-depth report. Miller said he planned to first stop by to pick up Tiarra and they would join him there. As Miller was assisting Tiarra down her front steps, she abruptly stopped, gasped and whispered, "Shh." Miller followed her gaze to yet another funeral in progress across the street. She then closed her eyes and said, "She's so very sorry she did it. She was only trying to protect her child." Tiarra unexpectedly swooned and Miller caught her in his burly arms, easing her into a sitting position on the steps.

"Tiarra—what is it? Who are you talking about?" Miller felt her transcended emotions.

Tiarra seemed to be slightly short of breath, so Miller waited patiently for her composure. She finally said, "I'm not sure, but I heard those words clear as a bell. It's a woman, Miller. A woman did it."

Miller looked perplexed. "Are you sure you weren't just picking up on a party-line conversation or something? I mean, how do you know it was related to the Lorence case?"

"I just do. C'mon—help me up. I'm anxious to hear the coroner's report."

Stan Stefanik invited them all to sit and handed out copies of his report. "Thith ith a little complicated. I'll try to eggthplain it ath betht ath I can. Pleath feel free to interrupt if you have a quethtyun." Ed had already started flipping through the pages and I could see his head tremors were back. Stan continued. "Ath I previouthly reported, there were multiple chemicalth that needed to be analythed. I will thtart with the leatht lethal trathe elementh found and lead to what wath the deadly dothe. Firtht, very thmall amount of arthenic were found, which can be found in all type-th of pethtithide-th. Did Rena complain of headache-th or dithineth? Did her breath thmell like garlic rethently?"

Ed actually laughed out loud and they all looked at him in shock. "I'm sorry—sorry—really—I just had to laugh. Rena and I ate garlic in our meals almost every night. I don't know if her breath ever would smell like anything else. I know my reaction was inappropriate. Again, I'm sorry." He paused a few seconds. "On the headache front, she usually complained of tension headaches. They always seemed to be relieved with a martini or soak in the hot tub—usually both."

"Yeth, well, we'll get to the martini glath in a moment. Thecondly, we found organophothphate-th, carbamate-th and thodium monofluoroathetate-th. Thethe are in variouth rodentithide-th and inthectithide-th. Eggthternal contact might have cauthed a rath—her thkin to break out—but nothing like that wath found during the autopthy. However, Rena did have mutated thellth in her lungth, heart, brain, liver and kidneyth. Thith would indicate thmall dotheth were ingethted over a two- to three-month period. Had Rena complained of nauthea, diarrhea or weight loth?"

Ed stifled his mirth this time and now they were all scowling at him. "Again—listen, I'm truly sorry. It's just that Rena would have thought it amusing that any woman would ever think to complain of weight loss. That was just her sense of humor. But, no, she didn't. She was pretty tough when it came to her aches and pains. She really didn't complain much. I just can't fathom that these chemicals were found in her system."

Stan said, "Common houthhold pethtithide-th like THEVIN have theeth compoundth."

Miller added, "CSI didn't find any such products at the Lorence residence, Stan. They had to have been introduced elsewhere."

"Pothibly. However, thum-one thpiked Rena'th martini that night with a lethal concoc—brew. The crime team found a deadly blend of ANTU and thuper-warfarin, both of which are rodentithide-th. I would tell you what ANTU thtandth for, but I have too hard a time pronounthing it. It'th thpelled out in the report. Lathtly, but thertainly not leatht, we found curare. Curare ith an eggthtremely deadly poithon thath been around thinth the early 1800th. Rena thuffered a progrethive paralythith, probably aware of what wath happening but unable to thpeak and therefore unable to call for help. Then, athphygg—inability to breathe. Finally, internal bleeding and cardiac arretht. I'm thorry, Ed. Rena thertainly thuffered a long and horrible death—poor girl."

Ed's eyes slowly filled with tears as they all watched his final and much more somber reactions to this nightmarish report. Ed definitely didn't find any more humor in the findings. He was beginning to look catatonic. Tiarra, for the most part, had sat silently with her eyes closed. Miller wondered at one point whether she had fallen asleep but she assured him she was making connections. He just hoped she hadn't dialed the wrong number. Miller eventually stood up and said, "Ed—meet me back at my office. We need to have another talk…"

Chapter 40

In an attempt to avoid having to remove my shoes again, I knocked at the Derrows' back door, which opened just off the kitchen—the servant's entrance, so to speak. I gave a terse wave to Louis, who was in the yard with the gardener, Armando. I could hear the old bastard grunting out orders—yeah, like he knows what he's talking about. 'Armando—you must be a very patient man,' I thought. Selma answered the door and ushered me in with a quick introduction to Alena, their housekeeper, who also happened to be Armando's wife. "Nize to meet you, Rrrena. Now, Mizzuz D., doan you frrret. Everrrything is under contrrrol." Alena's tongue and palate performed together like the Cirque du Soleil.

"Oh, Alena—what would I ever do without you." Alena quickly disappeared into another room and then out the door. I had noticed she was wearing bedroom slippers though Selma had on a pair of red Prada flats.

"Well, where's my walking companion hiding today?" I asked, with hopes of escaping before Louis came in. I took a quick peek out the window and saw he was grumpily filling a birdbath. Armando was at the far end of the yard quite skillfully lopping a shrub into a poodle-shaped topiary.

"Rena, I'm sorry to tell you this but Bernard is still at the vet. I would have cancelled but I really just need someone to talk to. Alena is going to be taking Louis to a doctor appointment in a couple of minutes so I thought I could persuade you to stay for a cup of tea and a piece of cake. I'll still pay you for your time."

'Good deal,' I thought. 'Cake *and* cash.' "Sure, Selma—I'd love to visit awhile." She invited me into the dining room and I took a seat. I suddenly realized the shoe rule must be Mr. Derrow's. She fussed in the kitchen for a few minutes and presented a lovely chocolate Bundt cake with raspberry sauce and a pot of tea. "This is such a treat for me, Selma. I could use a nice break like this."

"Oh, no, Rena—believe me, it's all my pleasure. You must think I'm silly but I just don't have anyone to talk to anymore. When I first met you, I felt so comfortable—a real connection. I usually don't have an opportunity to do this but since the dog is at the vet and Louis is gone, I couldn't help pass it up." I smirked to myself, thinking 'You mean Bernard at the vet and the dog gone.' She continued. "Well, it's just that Louis can be such an old codger at times. He's alcoholic, you know. I've put him into the hospital a few times for detox, but he always falls off the wagon. He can be so mean when he's drunk—it's stifling at times. I do try to keep the booze locked up. I allow him two cocktails a day and a glass of wine with dinner but he always finds a way to get more. He usually will invite the neighbors over to join us. He knows I won't confront him in front of company."

It was really way too much information, but I felt so horrible for her. Despite her tale of woe, she sure made a kickass Bundt. I had to ask, "So why do you stay with him?"

She sighed more than once. "You might think I'm a bit shallow but I'm quite happy with my lifestyle. I've always liked the finer things in life and usually want multiples of everything. Louis gives me what I want. I could never have that if I were on my own."

I thought how terribly sad she was as I swallowed that scrumptious last bite. "So, despite his 'codgerly' ways, you're okay—I mean, no physical bruises, right?"

"Oh, my, no—not to worry. Louis is usually too drunk to even move.

It's his words that knock me for a loop. I'm sorry for laying this on you, Rena. I just felt the need to vent."

"No problem, Selma. We all need to do that once in a while." Selma and I continued to chat about the less serious side of life and I found it was easier than expected to make her smile and laugh. "Shall I call before coming for the next visit?"

"No, Rena. Just come whether Bernard is here or not. I promise you'll be paid. I always have baked goodies, plus I could definitely use a good laugh…"

Chapter 41

Miller was reading Ed the riot act. "Listen, Ed. I really don't believe you killed Rena but you sure aren't making a good case for yourself—I mean, really—laughing during the coroner's report?"

"Jesus, I know, Miller. I just couldn't help it. Maybe I was nervous. Maybe I'm in denial. Who the hell knows?"

"Well what do you think of Tiarra's latest hunch about the killer being a woman? I've pretty much ruled out Tiffany Duffer and Jamie Fagioli. Were there any other women pet owners she dealt with? From her files, it didn't seem like Rena had very many clients in this new field of hers, especially just checking the last six months."

Ed replied, "The wife of Judge McGillacuddy is the only other woman I can think of, but it was longer than six months ago that Rena was involved with them. Besides that, she's completely bonkers and I doubt capable of something like this. I'm still a little suspicious of Tiarra and especially of her so-called abilities. She really makes my skin crawl but, again, it's been over the six-month time line. The only other thing I can think of is that Rena visited many of the local shelters, vet hospitals and pet stores to hold clinics, but I can't imagine how or why someone from any those places would have motive. To tell you the truth, I don't think it was a woman. The more I thought about what you said that first day we met—about the people I bring home from the shelter—I've been wary of Gus. After all, he was there that evening. His story about his reason for being homeless has been eating at me—it seems half-baked. But the thing is, he went to bed early that night shortly after Rena got home and I'm positive I would have known if he got up again. I'm a very light sleeper. I've thought about that evening over and over again. I had already eaten dinner with Gus that night because Rena had an extremely long schedule that day, plus she wanted to catch a yoga class. As a matter of fact, she went right to the hot tub and soaked for about an hour, then did paperwork for a while. By the time she was done with that, it was almost 10 p.m. She then got the martini I had made for her earlier out of the freezer and started to fix herself dinner. I turned in at that time and she hadn't eaten yet. I don't know. I don't really think Gus did it but the martini glass—did CSI check the liquor cabinet?"

"Yes, they took all of your gin, vodka and vermouth for processing— all negative for the compounds found in her system and no fingerprints matching Freeman's. You could be right about Gus though. I'll get over to the shelter to question him again. How about Elisha? When was she at your house last?"

"Oh, wow—I think it's been at least six or seven months. She's been keeping herself very busy at both the clinic and shelter. There's just no way she has anything to do with this—I've known her way too long.

"What about Lydia?" Miller surprisingly asked.

"What *about* Lydia?" Ed responded defensively.

"Well, I don't know. Were there any tensions or jealousies between the sisters? Just how close was she to Rena?"

"God, no, Miller. Lydia and Rena grew up with four brothers. They were the only sisters—meaning they were *very* close."

"Lydia and Rena? Lydia first—Rena second?" Miller knew he was reaching but had to see how Ed would react to the accusation.

"Don't even go there, Miller. Rena and I had a perfect marriage. And as for Lydia, she is happy in her own life. I can't believe you are even doing this to me." Not only was Ed sick to his stomach but his blood was starting to boil. "I want you to concentrate on all the nutcases out there, Miller, and find the person who has turned my life inside out."

"Okay, Ed. I believe you. You've got to understand my position in this. I need to look at all angles. I'm sorry if I've added to your grief. It must feel like you're stuck in a bad movie."

"It's getting to feel more like a series of bad movies…"

Chapter 42

I saw that Ralph's car was parked around the side of his building again where it couldn't be seen from his apartment. I pulled in right next to that Linda Blair puke-colored piece of scrap metal, stepped up to the window and peered inside. I frankly didn't care who saw me—sort of. It didn't take long to determine that Ralph had no special hand controls but I was willing to bet anything that he sponged up the funds in the pretense of having them installed. I had to walk around the building a few times to bring my boil down to a simmer.

Ralph seemed to be almost manic when he let me in. He was jubilant but in a nervous sort of way. His face was rosy and his lips were glued in a lecherous smile. "Well," he said, "I guess I'll get going and leave you two buddies to your therapy. It's a great day, don't you think?"

It was a great day for March that's for sure—bright, blue, cloudless sky and mild. I had to wonder, though, why Ralph would be so ecstatic about the weather. "Yes, Ralph, it is a great day. Are you heading out?"

"You bet! I've got some errands to do and then check in on Mom. Are you taking Moose for a walk today?"

"Definitely, but I thought I'd do a little stretching inside before his walk." I hesitated as Ralph got ready to leave and then said, "We probably should talk one of these days soon about how much longer you think you'd want my services."

"You're doing such a great job, Rena, I would hate to see it come to an end. You and Moose belong together!"

I thanked him for the nice comments and, with fingers crossed behind my back, told him to be safe as he popped a wheelie on his way out the door. 'Check on *"Mom"* my ass. What the hell could *he* possibly be so happy about?' I thought. I proceeded to Ralph's bedroom, keeping mindful of the wide-angle range. As I was finishing up with Moose, I made a quick scan of the wall in front of the bed. I didn't want to stare, knowing I was being filmed, but I noted there were three Impressionist-like prints that could easily hide the lens recording Ralphie boy's very own "reality TV" show. Moose and I headed out toward the elevator. It struck me that it probably would be best to grab a few of those videotapes now than later, just in case Ralph came home in between his *"errands"* and *"Mom"* checking. We quietly entered "STORAGE" and then Ralph's unit. The multitudes of videos were neatly stacked along six shelves, three on either side of the unit. None of the tapes were labeled. I decided to take three random tapes so as not to leave a big gap anywhere. I made sure to wear my oversized, zip fleece jacket today for comfortable video heisting and planned to put them in the trunk of my car immediately. I shut the light, locked the unit and, as I reached for the door to the hall, it flew open, smacking me in the head hard enough to make me see stars. My knees buckled and I dropped to the floor, holding my head in place so it wouldn't fall off my shoulders. It took several seconds before the room stood still. Moose was growling, taking a protective stance beside me, even though he could see it was Ralph. I could feel a lump forming on my forehead. Shakily, I said, "Ralph, what are you doing here?"—the *nerve* of me.

"What am *I* doing here? What are *YOU* doing here?"

I cautiously checked to make sure the videos were still well concealed under my sheepish fleece. "Well, I was—OW," I cried as I stood up, protracting my storytelling time by a few seconds. "I came in to turn off the alarm so I could test Moose on the back flight of stairs. One of the other tenants showed me what to do the other day." I looked up at the alarm switch, which was already switched to "OFF." "See?" I said, trying to focus my index finger in that direction.

Ralph followed the line of projection, his cheeks an even brighter candy-apple red than before. "Oh—yes—I see." He backed his wheelchair out of the doorway. I wondered in my fog why the alarm had already been turned off and why Ralph had returned. I switched the alarm back on and Moose stayed at my heels as we got out of there.

"I'm sorry, Ralph. I'm going to have to postpone the stairs and my walk with Moose today. My head is killing me."

Ralph looked at the egg poaching on my forehead and said, "Geez, Rena—I'm really sorry. It's just that I have to swing the door in hard like that to make it through with my chair. You better go home and get some rest. You're starting to look like part of a freak show…"

Chapter 43

Elisha met Miller at a nearby diner at his request so they could be away from the eyes and ears of the shelter and clinic. He had already prodded the rest of the staff at each of those places about Elisha and, in their eyes, she was nothing slight of an angel. He only half-suspected her in the first place but felt he should have a talk with her again, hoping she could shed more light on the Lorence household. She had, after all, been the longest of Ed's clinic-related acquaintances. Elisha arrived in a muted multi-colored gauze skirt and maize ruffled blouse, a lovely outfit and way too youthful for her age but somehow fitting. "Miller—so nice to see you again. How's the investigation coming?"

Off the cuff, Miller asked Elisha if she had ever been in trouble with the law. "Well, I don't know if this is the kind of trouble you mean, but—yes, I was. It was when we lived in Bohemia. It was late in the evening and I had been studying in the front room for a while. A strange car had pulled up on our dead-end street not too far from the house and parked there for almost an hour. At that time, there was only one other house at the beginning of the street and woods behind us. I kept an eye on the car and started getting nervous, thinking that maybe someone was planning to rob us. I got my shotgun and let off a round in the air to scare him off. He left in a hurry but, about ten minutes later, our house was surrounded by police. They kicked in the front door and shoved me against the wall in our foyer to cuff me! It turned out that the guy I shot over was a cop on break. No charges were filed. That guy must have shit his pants when that blast woke him. We all got a pretty big yuck out of that one—except for the cop, I'm sure."

Miller knew by her manner that she was a woman very comfortable in her own skin. She may have had a rough life but she was at peace with herself now and certainly not guilty of murder. They talked awhile in general and in as much depth as feasible about the Lorences and their life together. Miller was unable to unearth anything more than what had already surfaced. Since Elisha had voiced—*over and over and over again*—that "if there is anything I can do to help, just ask," Miller decided to enlist her in a safe and unobtrusive way. Miller asked her to simply observe Gus whenever possible, suggesting she take notes relating to his activities, whereabouts or anything she deemed extraordinary. "Oh, that'll be easy for me. I keep an eye on him all the time as it is. I truly don't trust that man, Miller. He's very elusive—puts on a good act though. I've seen him fool some of the doctors at the clinic, convincing them to write him prescriptions for pain pills and God knows what else. Then I watch him at the shelter. If that man is in pain, then I'd have to declare that the others at the clinic are near ready for their earth baths. I tell you, Miller—he's acting. After all—as a carny, I should know."

"Elisha, I'm not sure you realize the importance of what I'm asking you. You must be discreet and keep good notes—don't rely on memory. Even the best investigators can forget important details. And please be very careful—don't put yourself in any tight spots. Gus is a suspect in Rena Lorence's murder."

"Gus—a murderer? Oh, Miller, when I said I didn't trust him, I simply meant he was a liar, not a murderer. You don't really think he killed Rena, do you?"

"Elisha, I don't know what to think. There aren't many clues in this case. We know Rena was poisoned. So we know the what, where and when—it's the who, why and how that we still need to figure out. Do you have access to any of the residents' rooms at the shelter without raising eyebrows?"

"Sure, Miller. I have access to all the rooms. I assist with trash pickup and communion every week."

"Trash pickup and communion?"

"Oh, they're two very distinct activities. The pastor comes by once a week to serve communion to those who can't make it to the weekly mass." Elisha suddenly burst into laughter. Miller just stared, wondering whether she was stable enough to really trust her with his assignment. "Ha! Trash and communion—good one, Miller! I get it!" Miller just shook his head but couldn't help smile and laugh along with Elisha. She seemed just a pinch away from the nearest psych ward but, all in all, she was probably saner than most. "So what exactly should I be looking for, Miller?"

"Well, specifically, check to see if Gus has any kind of pesticide in his room—you know, anything that could be labeled as a poison. I don't want you to touch anything—just observe. Also try to note if he has any written materials lying around that relate to poisons, especially curare. You understand what I'm looking for, right?"

"Sure, Miller—things like D-Con, SEVIN, Round-up and deadly arrows—anything that might kill rats, insects, weeds or people—got it."

"This is my baby, Elisha, so if you think anyone is the least bit wary of your movements, stop what you're doing and contact me ASAP."

"Right—become suspect, abort, tell the father of the baby—got it. Sounds like a torrid love affair gone wrong."

Miller just stared into Elisha's bright, old eyes and wondered exactly what went on in there...

Chapter 44

I watched the three videos that I confiscated from Ralph's with immense concern. It seems Ralph had quite a constant bevy of babes to appease him. The first tape I viewed consisted of two episodes featuring two different women, both of whom seemingly were quite ready and willing to play "hide the salami" with him until he playfully jangled the cuffs and shackles at them. He spent a considerable time gently trying to persuade them to change their minds, but they both walked out without incident. The next show, however, was spectacularly lewd, one which I had to watch through split fingers a good part of the time. This woman was more than willing to entertain Ralph, fitting into his S&M theme with zeal. It looked like Ralph had found his true love. I mused how many it must have taken for him to cuff to that center finial before it finally snapped. I surmised that the last of the tapes probably involved this same trollop and almost didn't bother to play it. But hell, since I went through all that trouble to borrow the three tapes, I reasoned I might as well make another batch of popcorn—sans butter, of course.

The last show did not involve the kinky slut at all. It was Sandy—

Sandy, the CVS clerk. She seemed extremely shy and it took a lot of coaxing on Ralph's part plus several glasses of wine later to get her between the sheets. During her first visit and what explicitly was deemed to be her sexual debut, Ralph didn't restrain her as in his previously filmed style. But when the scene cut to what appeared to be a different day, based on my observation of the stripping of distinct garments and the angle of sunlight in the room, Sandy hesitantly went along with him and allowed herself to be fettered. Ralph began on a gentle note, which actually did look like normal lovemaking, but it didn't take much time for his excitement to erupt into a love-razing. He frivolously spanked her hard but she soberly protested. Ralph protested her protest and that's when things went haywire. The more Sandy begged him to stop, the more wild-eyed and vulgar he became. His growing excitement was exacerbated as it melded with his swells of anger. The increasingly intense spanking, which had reddened all of Sandy's cheeks, ceased for a moment, long enough for Ralph to reach to the bottom drawer of his night stand and pull out a cat-o'-nine-tails. Catching sight of the whip, Sandy pleaded for her freedom. Maniacal Ralph only responded with a tight-lipped grin. He began his torment, Sandy's torso lifting and falling in a hellish, writhing rhythm. I couldn't believe my eyes. "You deranged piece of shit."

At this point, I had moved to the floor and sat smack in front of the TV screen like a little kid watching a horror movie, wanting to avert my eyes but unable to do so. I was startled and gasped in soprano when the center finial suddenly went flying. "Well, that answers that." Sandy could now at least sit up and use her arms, albeit as a unit. I was nauseated and knew I had to report what I was seeing. Ralph was like a metastatic malignancy on society. How would I even be able to face him again? The scene was now volatile. Sandy was fighting back, even though her ankles were still shackled. She hooked Ralph under his nose with the manacles in a defensive move, which caused him to reflexively reach up, flinging one of the tails of the whip over his shoulder, giving him a taste of his own medicine. He exhaled a throaty growl like a rabid animal and sharply threw his crop to the floor. "Oh, God—please just let her go," I quietly begged. Sandy sat there as painful sobs wracked her body. In a pathetically low tone, she pled with Ralph to let her go. Amazingly, he acquiesced, unlocking her hands and feet. She was weak and tried to scurry off the bed but was unsteady. As she stood, Ralph held her with one arm for a moment to keep her from falling. I could see she almost relaxed, yielding to his support. "Get the hell out of there!" I screeched in an Irish whisper. Just as quickly as those words left my mouth, Ralph had violently shoved Sandy into his bathroom. I could see in the dim light of that forbidden room that Sandy had drooped to the floor and appeared to be unconscious. Now I loudly shrieked as Ralph spun around and looked directly at the camera, giving himself a thumbs-up sign. "You crass fucking bastard. You wait, you mange. Your ass is grass and I'm the mower," I professed.

"Rena? You okay down there?" Oh, shit. I woke Ed up. I had the TV at its lowest volume but my thinking out loud had been exuberant this time.

"I'm fine, sweetie. Just watching one of my crime shows." I just couldn't let Ed know what I had done—he'd kill me. Boy, this menopause sure was making me behave strangely these days. "Go back to sleep, my love. I'll be up shortly." I was so glad he hadn't gotten out of bed. I had paused the tape when he yelled down. I didn't start it back up again until I heard him snoring.

The remaining film footage only lasted another minute at best. Ralph had quickly dressed and ran out of the room. The scene was still except for the diaphragmatic movements I could still detect with the ebb and flow of air from Sandy's lungs. At least she was still alive. Then the tape abruptly went black. I sat there alone in front of the snowy, shushing TV absolutely horrified but also intensely nettled. Could that have all been just an act? I doubted it. Sandy didn't look like the type of girl that would coddle to Ralph's whims. And now that the tape had stopped, I wondered if she truly was still alive. Now what—who could I tell without getting into trouble myself? There was only one person that came to mind who had loads of patience, understanding, intelligence and insight…

Chapter 45

"So, what did you think at the coroner's the other day?" Miller had dropped by Tiarra's out of the blue for a heart-to-heart. "Any suspicions about Ed?"

"No, Miller—not at all. That was just all nervous behavior. Ed wouldn't hurt a fly. But I *do* have something new to tell you."

"More visions?"

"Yes, and I'm sticking with my earlier prediction that it was a woman. I keep hearing her say, 'mea culpa, mea culpa,'"

"That's Latin, isn't it?"

"Yes—it means 'it's my fault' or 'I am to blame.'"

"Again, though—how do you know it's related to Rena's case?"

"Trust me on this, Miller—I just do. Keep checking out the women she was involved with over the past two months."

"Tiarra, believe me—I've questioned them all—at least all the ones that were on her schedule over the past six months and, remember, the coroner said the trace elements found in Rena's system would not have been ingested any time prior to the past three months at best."

"Well, maybe you should talk with Ed again. What about female family members or friends?"

"If you feel that strongly about it, I'll question Ed again…"

Chapter 46

"Sweetie? I need your advice." It was the morning after I watched Sandy's beating. I wondered how strongly Ed would react to what I was about to tell him. "Please try not to be upset with me," I urged as I slowly batted my lashes, trying to look serious and sexy all at once.

Ed was scowling as he walked toward me. He reached up and grazed my forehead with two fingers. I recoiled. "What the hell happened here?"

"Well, the bump on my head is all part of what I'm about to tell you."

Ed now sensed my high anxiety. His dark scowl lightened and he covered my shoulders with his warm arm like a shawl. "You know you can tell me anything, my baby doll. C'mon—sit over here by me."

We sat and snuggled for a few seconds on the couch before I introduced this inconceivable tale. I struggled for the words to begin. "Well—you know how much I love forensics and like to fantasize I'm part of a CSI team when I'm at a client's house?"

As I began this difficult uphill climb, the red in Ed's face gradually rose and loomed like the Rockies while his calm slowly eroded like the Grand Canyon. All he could choke out was "Yeah?"

"Well—I sort of stumbled upon something that I think really is criminal and I'm just not sure how to handle it."

"Holy shit, Rena! *What?*"

I went on to explain about Ralph and then proceeded to show him the films. Ed's tide of emotions was quickly becoming a tsunami. "That licentious *bastard*," he roared. I didn't know what licentious meant, but knew it wasn't good seeing how it was teamed with 'bastard.' "Rena—you *have* to tell the authorities."

"But, Ed—I—um—snuck into his storage unit and stole the tapes. Well, actually borrowed—like my own personal BlockBusters." I tried to don a smile.

"This is no time to joke, Rena. If he ever finds out you took them, you could be next."

"Well, I *do* plan on returning them."

"Stay the hell out of that storage room!"

"Okay, Ed—I know—I'll talk with Judge McG.—he'll know exactly what I should do…"

Chapter 47

"Ed—I spoke with more than a dozen people at the shelters, hospitals and pet stores where Rena has worked and there's not one person I would consider suspect. Tiarra is still convinced it was a woman, but I'm really not all that sure since she really hasn't proven anything to us yet. I'm wondering if Rena might have had *anyone* in her circle of family or friends who may have had a beef with her."

"Miller—I'm telling you again—she and her family were very close and, truthfully, she's been too damned busy to see any of her old friends. The only person you haven't spoken with yet is Judge McGillacuddy. Even though it's been well over six months since she had his llama—believe it or not—under her care, she did continue to visit with him and his nutty wife. Rena lovingly called him Judge McG. and they became great buddies. And, despite his wife's lunacy, Rena seemed to love her too. I really don't think either of them is culpable, nor do I think Rena even saw them all that often, but maybe the judge could add something worthwhile. Truthfully, Miller, I just don't feel sure about much of anything anymore. Rena sure seemed to have a stockpile of secrets."

"I'm sure it wasn't intentionally to hurt you, Ed. You have to remember that the poisons were affecting her mental health and behaviors…"

Chapter 48

I called the McGillacuddys' veterinarian prior to my next visit. He advised that Lulu wasn't at all tone deaf. The problem was that she was plainly and simply deaf. For some reason, the judge couldn't quite accept that diagnosis. The vet said that a little extra attention to Lulu wouldn't hurt and asked that I just humor all of them for a few weeks. He added that the judge could definitely use a distraction.

As I pulled in to the long and winding, spruce-lined driveway at the farm, I saw Mrs. Mc—I mean, Lady Buggé—heading toward the barn. She was wearing an enormous, floppy red hat, a ruffled, red and white polka-dot blouse and denim bib overalls, nicely accented with red pumps. 'Great outfit, Lady Buggé,' I thought as I laughed out loud in the car. 'Perfect color coordination.' The judge had approached my car before I had time to compose myself.

"I take it you just caught a glimpse of MaryLou? That's okay—she gives me a good chuckle now and again, too."

"She certainly is a character, Judge," I gushed and then hoped that wasn't too bold or insulting.

"She's a full-blown *cast* of characters, Rena!" Judge followed that statement with a bellowing laugh. I felt much better now.

I stepped out of my car and Judge McG. looked at me worriedly. "What happened to your head?"

"My head?" I had tried to block it out of my mind, but reaching up and feeling above my brow, I queasily said, "Oh—I got hit with a door—I'm fine."

"You certainly don't look fine to me," he scowled. "You look rather frazzled." Guess the ice and concealer hadn't quite done the trick.

"Well, Judge—I do need some legal advice. Do you have a few extra minutes?" My thoughts had been so disjointed since watching the videos and talking with Ed. I hadn't really formulated any questions. This was all happening rather impromptu.

"Shoot."

"Well, is it illegal to shackle someone to your bed, even though they were willing, and then beat the crap out of them?" Boy, did *that* come out wrong. "I mean, can someone take a video of someone else in their own home without the other person knowing? Or, how about filming someone while they're working without their permission?" My questions seemed so helter-skelter.

"Whoa, Rena—hold up. What exactly is it you're trying to tell me?"

The words and pictures whirled in my brain like a cyclone. Before I could warn the judge to take shelter, they were spilling out of my mouth in a torrent. 'Auntie Em!' After making me slow down, twice repeat my story and answer a few simple questions, Judge sighed. He raised one brow, while squinting the opposite eye and said, "That's one humdinger of a mess you're in, Rena." He looked at the ground and shook his head. "You're most definitely going to need help in putting that maggot away."

When he ended that sentence, I burst into tears. I was so relieved—I had purged, spilled the beans, tattled, ratted. Had I opened Pandora's box? What had I done? I cried even harder. Judge cradled me in his arms like a baby and my fear tapered. "If anything, the videos certainly prove he's not paralyzed, right?"

"Do you have the tapes with you?"

"You betcha. I was planning on putting them back, but this guy needs to be exposed—so to speak." Judge didn't snicker. This was way too serious.

"Rena, this woman—Sandy—she could be dead for all we know. This guy sounds terribly dangerous. There needs to be an investigation, and now. I'll make some calls. I'm going to keep these tapes for review. The first thing we can do is see if Sandy is still employed at one of the CVS stores. You continue to treat this guy's dog, but do not—I said **DO NOT**—go back into that storage area. I'll make sure you don't get into any trouble. You just make sure you don't get yourself killed. Is there anything else you should be telling me?"...

Chapter 49

Miller was back out at our house for two reasons: one, he wanted to comb through my desk and files again and, two, to discuss Ed's conversation with Dom Modigliani.

"I recently found out some things about Rena, Miller—things she had never told me. They may be insignificant to the case but were remarkable to me in that Rena and I never kept secrets. When I met with Mr. Modigliani, he told me that he and Rena always went to the cemetery where his wife is buried to have lunch and for her to treat his Jack Russell. I was really shocked that she never told me that. Rena and I always loved visiting old cemeteries together. Even when she was in college, we would go to our favorite one so I could help her study in peace and quiet."

"Maybe she didn't say anything because that had been something special between the two of you. She probably just didn't want to hurt your feelings."

"Rena knew me better than that. I would *never* have been hurt knowing that, but I'm totally disheartened knowing it after the fact. But that's not all of it. The other thing that actually alarmed me was that Dom told me

Rena was at his bakery the day police nabbed his wife's murderer—he said it was the day before Rena died. Why wouldn't she have *told* me about that?"

"That *is* pretty strange that she didn't mention it, Ed, but I don't think these things have any relevance to the case. And—remember—the poisons were probably having an effect on her memory over the final weeks."

"I realize that, Miller, but I do find it all disturbing. It just makes me wonder what else she failed to mention which might be relevant."

"Well, unfortunately, we'll never know. I do need to go through her files again though. One thing that seems to be missing is a day planner of some sort. She must have kept track of her daily schedule, right?"

"Yes, of course she did. She had to keep strict time limits—otherwise, she'd never get home. It was a pocket-sized calendar, I think. Wasn't it in her bag?"

"No, I never found one. Where do you think she would have kept it?"

"Pocket calendar? Pockets, Miller—come on! This might take a while—there is a whole closet that was exclusively for Rena's coats, jackets and footwear..."

Chapter 50

I had a bewildering sense of gloom about visiting Selma again, but some mysterious force pulled my car into the Derrow driveway once more. I contrived a plan to get Selma out of the house in the event Bernard was still not back. I would ask her to come to the vet's office with me so that I could at least meet the dog with the cork up its ass. That way she could escape from her cantankerous husband for at least a short while. I reluctantly walked to the door and rang the bell. I was somewhat relieved when Alena answered.

"Rrrena, dearr. We werre expecting you. Come, come." And, in a whisper, she added, "Take off yourr shoes—yes?"

It was only two in the afternoon, but it looked as if cocktail hour had begun at the Derrow household. Armando, Alena and another couple were there, all with drinks dutifully in hand. Selma rose from her oxbow chair and graciously took my arm in an attempt to sweep me into the kitchen but, like an old church organ, Louis piped up and bellowed, "Come in here and sit down! Have a drink—don't be so antisocial."

'Pompous ass,' I thought.

140

"Oh, Louis," Selma sweetly said. "Yes, Rena—do come in and meet our friends." With a polite, queen-like wave of her hand toward the couple, she said, "These are our neighbors—Floyd and Fauna Forester."

We all shook hands and then Selma politely asked, "What can I get you to drink, Rena?"

I normally never drank during the workday and especially before 5 p.m. but, if I had to deal with the abrasive Louis Derrow, I'd need something to soothe the chafing. I equated it to applying aloe after a bikini wax. "A glass of Chardonnay would be nice—thanks." I suddenly realized there was no sign of Bernard again.

After about ten minutes of sipping and small talk, Armando and Alena suddenly stood, announced they had much to do, excused themselves and left. They were both wearing slippers. I then noted that the Derrows and Foresters were wearing designer leather shoes—natch. I swilled the rest of the glass and Selma filled it before I could properly refuse. I could see Louis was already three sheets to the wind, even before his mouth opened. We were all beginning to feel a little edgy in his company.

"I just can't say enough about Armando and Alena," Louis surprisingly slurred. "They'd do just about anything for us." He almost looked like he was about to cry. Then, more in character, "Too bad they're such dull people—no education—no class—lowest rung on the social ladder. They're lucky I even hired them," he brusquely announced.

I knew it was too good to last. "You don't really believe you're better than they, do you?" I nervously scolded.

"Of course I do! Any idiot could see why! I'm the smartest person you're ever going to meet, young woman. I could have gotten into any college I wanted—Harvard, Yale…" His voiced trailed off and he continued to mumble about his superiority as he numbly gazed into his near-empty glass. We all sat dumbfounded.

This conversation was going nowhere but downhill and fast. Louis loudly gulped the rest of his Scotch and handed the empty glass to Selma.

With that, Floyd and Fauna leapt out of their seats, made their excuses and left posthaste. On the other hand, I was starting to feel a little feisty and thought I'd stick it out a while longer.

Selma looked pleadingly at "His Highness" and said, "Why don't you wait until we eat, Louis. Take a short nap while I'm preparing dinner."

"Why don't you just get me one more drink!" Louis's combative tone stole my spunk. "Get me that drink—my jaw is killing me!" Then he looked at me and said, "You should know what's wrong with my jaw! What can I do for it?"

Selma quickly explained Louis's jaw problem and flitted off to the kitchen.

"Well, sounds like you have TMJ syndrome. You probably grind or clench your teeth."

"Of course I clench my teeth, living with that fucking cunt!"

I heard a pop and felt my eyeballs resting on my cheekbones. His tirade continued.

"I've been married to that bitch for twenty-five years and we haven't had sex for twenty-two of them! My jaw is always clenched! Why the hell do you think I drink?"

My body was slinking down into a lump, trying to become a throw pillow or at least blend in with the fabric. How would I ever extricate myself from this one? I glanced toward the kitchen and wondered whether I should wait for Selma to come back or just make a run for it. I just hoped she couldn't hear what he had just said, though I was pretty sure she'd heard it all before. She re-entered the room and handed Louis his drink. He scoffed something unintelligible and she sat down. I could see his thorny mood was spiking. He was most definitely a prick, in every sense of the word. I hoped he'd pass out soon. His double chin rested on his chest momentarily and then he lifted his head. His eyes were spiteful and held Selma like a vise. His barrage resumed.

"You're a stupid woman, Selma—a stupid, stupid woman!" On and on he went and with each caustic remark, she held her head higher. All she said was, "Yes, Louis."

I couldn't listen to it any longer. I ran out of the house, shoes in hand. Selma calmly walked out a respectable thirty seconds later, her head still held high. I was the one in tears, not her. I couldn't believe her composure. My only comment to her was "How can you live like this?"

She sighed, handing me a container of cookies, taking her time in answering. "Not to worry, dear—he won't remember anything in the morning."

"No," I sniffled, "but you will…"

Chapter 51

"Tell me everything you remember about that day." Miller had decided to check out the whole story behind the murder of Dom's wife. Dom had just finished describing the day of the murder and the undercover surveillance thereafter. The apprehension was really quite simple.

"Not'a too much'a to tell'a—just that'a Rena an'a I come'a back to'a store from'a cemetery. She wanna' come in'a for a loaf'a bread'a. We walk in'a door an'a they were'a cuffin'a guy'a. He had'a some'a balls to come in an'a try to buy a cannoli. Our man'a spot'a him right away an'a haul'a his ass out'a here'a."

"Did the murderer say anything to Rena?"

"Yeah—he said'a he really wanted'a that'a cannoli. I yell at'a him'a. I say'a, 'You don'a talk'a to my Rena, you filt'y bastard'a! You go an'a rot in'a hell'a!'"

Dom provided both the names of the nabbed and nabber. "Well, I'm glad they got him, Mr. Modigliani. It must help you in some small way. Thank you for your time."

"My'a pleasure."

Miller sat in his car and contemplated whether or not to waste any time investigating Gina's murderer. He decided to hold off on that and instead visit another client of mine. He'd contact the arresting officer of the Modigliani case when he returned to the office.

Miller was amazed at the amount of driving involved between all of my clients. Close to an hour later, he arrived at Henri's. Ed had already spoken with Henri, but Miller felt the need to follow up.

Henri was conspicuously shaken when Miller introduced himself and advised he was there to talk about me. "Eet was an acc-zee-dent, Off-eecer. I will gladly pay for all zee damages. Just tell me what I owe, eh?" Henri caught the look on Miller's face and realized he was not referring to the easel debacle. He then fully confessed his sins in an emotional breakdown. "I only keesed her one time. Okay—two times, but zat was all. Eet was all so very ee-no-cent. I loved Rena—I would never hurt zat girl." Miller took some time to calm Henri so he could obtain a much clearer explanation. They talked for an hour or more, much longer than Miller had anticipated, but Henri had a charm that was certainly captivating and Miller could see how an innocent woman might be taken in. Miller had to laugh when Henri explained the incident at the art store but also felt that Henri may have had motive based on his feelings for unattainable moi. Too bad there was no other evidence to incriminate. Henri had allowed Miller to search his car and premises, vowing he had nothing to hide. By the time Miller left, he felt in his gut that Henri was not the cause of my misfortune.

As Miller was heading back to his car for the long drive back to his office, Henri called out, "Pleeze find zee scourge zat took our beautiful Rena."

Miller was tired. He sat in his car another moment trying to clear his tired eyes with drops of saline solution and straighten things out in his head. He was baffled. Where was his lead? He had studied my calendar and had investigated way beyond the three previous months. There was only one more client to speak with and that was McGillacuddy. There was another name but had no matching file. That name was Bernard, but Miller decided it must have been a cancelled appointment. He still had a few shelters and vets to visit. He was dreading so much that this case was going to culminate in Dead-endsville. Still sitting in his dark car in Henri's driveway, his cell phone startled him out of his deep thoughts but he answered the call calmly. "Miller."

"Miller, it's Ed. What's the word on your end?"

"I'm sorry, man—nothing really to report." Miller decided to keep Henri's advances quiet unless something more surfaced to go on. He'd spare Ed the added grief of learning another secret of mine.

"Well, I think I might have something—can you meet me for a drink at the Hofbrau on Warner's Lake?"

"Yeah—give me a half hour."

"I'll be waiting."

Miller started out driving in a light drizzle that before long morphed into a deluge. His wipers were at top speed and he could barely see. He inched along trying to stay focused on the double yellow center lines. The night was totally black with only an occasional flicker of light stemming from a distant farmhouse. There was an abrupt thump and Miller found his car swinging in a clockwise direction. When he stopped, he saw he had spun one hundred eighty degrees and was in the center of the road. He jumped out of the car and found a large doe on its side now directly in front of the car. "Jesus!" Miller slowly approached and saw the fear in her wide, dark eyes now reflecting his headlights. He could see the vapor of her disquieted breaths. The doe held Miller's eyes. Miller felt horrible and was about to get back in the car to call for help when the doe scrambled to her feet and slowly walked off into the woods, turning back once to look at Miller, almost as if to tell him not to worry—she'd be okay. Suddenly realizing the danger his car presented, though there had been no traffic at all, Miller rushed to move it off the road. The car squealed and moaned, but he got it safely off and onto the grass, partly in a ditch. The rear side panel had actually punctured his back tire. He called for service and then notified his office. He got the number for the Hofbrau in East Berne and paged Ed. "Listen—I hit a deer and my car is demo'd. I have to wait for service, but I'm going to really need a drink and a ride, so wait for me. I mean it—don't leave…"

Chapter 52

My RN friend, Michelle, answered Ralph's door and I could tell she was in a huff.

"Hey, Michelle—what's up?"

"Ralph's most recent home health aide quit. Someone from her family called the office yesterday and said she just up and moved. Can you believe it? We are so short-staffed right now." Michelle was exasperated and furiously trying to complete her paperwork.

Ralph was being relatively quiet and letting her rant.

"Well," I injected, "maybe Ralph doesn't really need an aide. I mean—you are very independent, right?" I could see the jab was effective. I was boldly holding his gaze, picturing bars in front of his face. I wondered how long it would take Ralph's cellmate to impose hard labor—literal penile servitude—he so deserved it.

Moose came loping out of the bedroom, his body performing a belly dance of happiness upon seeing me.

Michelle seemed to relax a moment when she saw me with Moose. "You two are great together."

"Yeah—Moose and I have bonded quite nicely. As a matter of fact, Ralph, I was going to ask if I could take him home for the weekend. I have a lot of land and thought it would be great for him to run free for a change. What do you think?"

"I don't see why not. Actually, that would be perfect. I have a lot going on and would have needed someone to watch him any way."

'I bet you do,' I thought, as visions of helpless women fighting for their lives crystallized in my mind. "Well, great—I'll bring him back Monday then."

Michelle said, "Well, I'm outta here. We'll see what we can do to get you another aide, but there might be a wait. See you next week."

"No rush," Ralph added. "As Rena has so astutely observed, I am fairly independent."

I thought I'd gag. I decided not to give him the pleasure of looking his way. Michelle scooted and I had a few decisions to make. "Are you going out today, Ralph?"

"I don't really feel like it, but, yes, I am. My mom really needs me and she seems pretty down in the dumps."

"Well, that's too bad. I think I'll do Moose's treatment here as usual and then just take him home. Is that okay?"

"That's fine. I'll be out of your hair in a minute." Ralph gathered a few things in a bag, said his good-byes and left. Looked like he'd be away the whole weekend.

I sat on the bed with Moose and started his treatment, acutely aware of the all-knowing lens. My skin began to crawl as goosebumps slowly rose, and the little hairs at the nape of my neck stood in a stiff dance as I envisioned Sandy's struggle for survival and heard her appeals. My stomach felt queasy but I quelled it by silently counting out five minutes as I put Moose to sleep with my rubdown. I ultimately said out loud, "Moose, honey—I'll be right back. I have to make a pit stop to the lobby." My voice sounded eerie as I performed for the camera. I left the room, grabbed the key and went down to the lobby. I used the bathroom and stepped outside for a breath of fresh air. Ralph's car was gone from his usual spot, but I walked around the side of the building to be sure he hadn't just moved it. Calmly, I walked back inside and took the stairs to the second floor. I headed straight for "STORAGE." For a split second I thought, 'Sorry, Ed—Sorry, Judge,' but I was compelled to do this. In double time, I entered and opened his unit. The camera's red "RECORD" light was winking at me. I pulled a clean tissue from my pocket and stopped the filming. I hustled out of there and returned to his apartment. Moose was still sawing wood. I opened the forbidden door to the bathroom. I felt malevolence in the umber shadows. With the tissue, I flipped the light switch. The room was grungy and foreboding. My eyes slowly scanned the room, coming to a dead stop at the far corner. There were streaks—drippings, actually. An attempt at wiping them from view or memory was apparent. Upon closer inspection, my underlying dread surfaced with the recognition of blood. I slowly turned my entire body, though my scanning became more manic like I had developed nystagmus. There on the wall next to the sink was a partial bloody hand print. That was enough. "Moose! Wake up! We're outta here, Bud!"

Moose sprung out of bed and ran to my side. "Wow! You *are* doing better! Let's go for a ride!"…

Chapter 53

Miller had to wait a good forty minutes before his tow came. For an extra sawbuck, the truck driver obliged by giving him a ride to the tavern. Ed was at the bar shooting the shit with one of the locals when Miller walked in.

"Jesus, Miller—you poor bastard. You look like a drowned rat."

"Yeah—thanks—I feel much better now." Miller ordered a boilermaker and peeled off his waterlogged sports jacket. "Got an extra room for another stray tonight?"

"Absolutely. I'll even give you a ride into town tomorrow."

"The roads sure are dark out here in these parts," Miller said in hick-ese.

"Yeah, you never know what might be lurking out there –skunk, possum, woodchuck," and in a whisper Ed said, "and when I say woodchuck, I'm talking about one of the native rubes." They laughed quietly. "Unfortunately, though, you met with one of the worst offenders."

"No shit!" and with that they both snickered loudly and downed a shot of whiskey. "You're really quite lucky, though," Ed said. I've heard horror stories about people being kicked to death after having one of those suckers crash through their windshield."

"Christ—what a way to go."

"Yeah—speaking of that, let's head back to my place so we can talk in private. I'll get you some dry clothes, a bite to eat and then we can really get hammered."

They drove the short distance back to our place in silence—both very contemplative. Once settled and dry, Miller said, "So, what is it, Ed? Something good I hope, 'cause I ain't gettin' squat from anyone else."

"I don't know why I didn't think to tell you this before, Miller, but less than a year ago, Rena was involved with a client who was arrested on insurance fraud charges. He was faking a paralysis and, based on home videos, was blown in. Rena was the one who found the tapes and reported him. He was also suspected of assault, kidnapping and murder based on the film footage plus all the blood that was found in his apartment. The blood was not his but no bodies were ever found. There were several women missing who had been involved with him, including a couple of home health aides from the visiting nurses. DNA obtained from the family of one of those aides matched blood evidence found on this guy's mattress including the flip side. He was finally charged with assault and suspected kidnapping after a family member ID'd their missing daughter from one of the videos. Plus, the sister of another missing woman made a positive ID of her sister from another tape, with her DNA matching one of the blood samples found. He's been held without bail based on the brutality shown in the videos, though his defense team is fighting it tooth and nail. They're basing their strategies on the following facts: no bodies, no motive. Plus the blood evidence obtained could simply be vaginal blood from first-time intercourse or menstruation. Also the videos could all have been staged. The judge in the case isn't buying it, though, and refuses to let him out. Rena was going to testify against this guy."

"Christ Almighty, Ed! This is huge! When was she going to testify?"

"Her testimony would have been this week."

"Who's the judge in this case, Ed?"

"Rathbone Hillcott."

"Why the hell didn't you tell me this earlier?"

"Shit, Miller—I don't know. Do you think maybe because *I'm grieving!*"

Miller eased up. "I'm sorry, man. It's just that this is very important. This must be the Walway case you're talking about, right?"...

Chapter 54

As Moose and I were rushing to escape the horrors in Ralph's apartment, we ran smack into a woman who was rushing headlong for his door and, boy, did she ever look pissed. She appeared to be in her mid-thirties, dressed in black spandex workout pants with a tight, white t-shirt on a body to just die for. Her shoulder-length, toffee-brown hair was tousled. She was quite sensual and my first impression was that she probably was one of Ralph's current (and surviving) film stars, though an intelligent confidence came through that didn't quite fit Ralph's type.

"Ralph's not home, if that's who you're looking for. I think he's gone away for the weekend—possibly much longer," I advised.

"I'm looking for my sister, Sandy. She's been missing for a few days. No one has heard from her at work. I found a message on her answering machine from this guy Ralph, who left his address for her." The initial raging river of anger shown by this striking woman was rapidly melting into a puddle of fear.

Taking care not to let her drag me overboard into her fast-rising emotional pool, I found my sea legs and held her gaze and shoulders firmly. "Listen," I started, trying to keep my voice steady, "we've got to get out of here. Just come with me and I'll try to explain." I grabbed her upper arm and she didn't resist. We started down the stairs when I suddenly remembered one minor detail. "Wait here for just one second— *please*—and keep an eye on the dog for me. I promise I'll be right back." I tore back up the stairs and sprinted to "STORAGE." My hands were shaking so hard that the key fell with a resounding chink on the old marble floor, the metallic sound scolding with a tsk-tsk, the echo slowly withdrawing down the hall like a punished child. I quickly tried again and succeeded, running to Ralph's unit. I restarted the "RECORD" process and made tracks out of there. Now back with the woman who had obediently waited with Moose, we raced to my car. She got in without hesitation. Between huffs of quickened breath, I said, "I'm Rena Lorence—an animal therapist. I've been taking care of Ralph's dog here—say hi to Moose. Over the past few weeks, I've discovered some gruesome things about Ralph. I'm on my way right now to speak to a judge. If you come with me, you can report your sister's disappearance."

"I'm definitely in," she said. "But just what do you mean by 'gruesome'? Do you know if Sandy is okay? I'll *kill* that bastard if he hurt my sweet, baby sister."

She had a soft toughness about her I really liked. I went on to explain about the videos without giving too much detail. I knew she'd find out soon enough. "I really don't know if Sandy is okay or not. We can only hope it won't take too long to find out." I didn't mention the bathroom discovery to her either but told her we'd discuss it all with the judge. "By the way," I said, "what's your name?"

"My name is Sophie—Sophie Williams."

"It's a real pleasure to meet you, Sophie."

She went on to tell me how she literally raised Sandy because their mother had died of breast cancer at a very young age. Sandy was only six at the time and Sophie was sixteen. Their dad worked two jobs to support them and basically drank himself to sleep every night. Sandy was in her last year of high school when he died from cirrhosis. Sophie clerked at a bank but was not pulling in enough pay for them to stay in their home. She knew she had to find a better job. She decided then that she would

153

become an exotic dancer. She developed her "gentleman's club" persona and became "Phantasy Sinwilling." She made great money at many of the upscale clubs and was able to pay for Sandy's college education, though she said Sandy could never make up her mind on a major. Sandy worked odd jobs in between semesters to help out. Her most recent job was as a cashier at CVS.

We had been driving for about ten minutes when my cell phone rang. It was Judge McG. "Judge! I was just on my way out to see you." I knew I had to be sensitive in my choice of words. "I have more—um—information for you, plus there's a young woman with me who wants to file a missing-persons report on her sister. She thinks she may have had contact with Ralph Walway."

"Turn your car around and meet me at the county DA's office. I'm on my way there now with the tapes." He hesitated, then said, "And what do you mean by 'more information'?"

"Well, Judge, let's just say hopefully enough to put this guy away for a long time. I'll save it for our meeting with the DA."

Judge McG. met us outside the county courthouse. By this time, we were all on pins and needles. We scrambled up three flights of stairs to the DA's office. He was expecting us and ushered us in to his modestly furnished office. Judge McG. led the introductions.

The DA was Albert P. Knower, a former town justice in rural Oneida County. He had also made his living as a farmer, which was clear by the size of his hands and the firmness of his old grizzly-bear shake. He had a slight twang when he spoke, like many of the rural upstate New York yokels.

First things first, DA Knower wanted to hear the whole story from the beginning. Judge McG. assured me that I'd have full immunity against any charges of wrongdoing. I started with my general but trained observations of Ralph and then went on to describing the day I had found the first tape Ralph used to prop open that side emergency door. "That tape clearly proves in the last segment that Ralph is in no way paralyzed, which led me to then check out the emergency exit he used. I discovered there was no elevator access. While checking that exit, I set off an alarm, which led to another resident of the apartment complex permitting me access to the storage area where the alarm could be turned off. The storage unit is where I—*ahem*—stumbled upon Ralph's cache of videos." I quickly spouted what I observed on the tapes I borrowed. My thoughts were a blizzard and my words struck them in squalls.

"Whoa! Hold on, young lady," D.A. Knower interjected. "The films don't prove anything unless we find a body."

"Please—hear me out." I reported Ralph's bathroom paranoia and his forbidden entrance there. Sophie looked frozen in terror. "Once I knew I could stop the filming and check out what he had deemed taboo, I couldn't resist." I went on to explain what I saw in that cold, tiled crypt. "I'm sure CSI could obtain enough DNA from the scene." Judge McG. lowered his head slightly, eyes lifted however, silently chiding me in a parental way with his wise yet caring gaze.

"Yes, love," D.A. Knower said, "but what do we have to compare that DNA with?"

Sophie had been very still up until now, her eyelids damming, the flood waters about to give way. Her speech was almost inaudible as the sounds escaped from her tightened throat. "I could give you DNA from my sister, Sandy. All I ask of you is to find her."

We watched the films then and I held Sophie close. Her energy seemed completely spent and she leaned limply against me. After the last tape had played through, I asked, "Is there sufficient evidence for a warrant?" Sophie, Judge and I looked pleadingly at D.A. Knower.

"We'll start with a search of Mr. Walway's apartment, storage unit and car. Pending our findings, we'll issue an arrest warrant. The very least we can charge him with is insurance fraud. With Sophie's help, we may be able to up the ante with harassment, stalking, assault and possibly kidnapping. Sophie, Hon, I want you to fill out your missing-persons report now."

Sophie was trembling but able to compose enough to function numbly. Judge and I told her we'd stay and give her any help she needed. Judge looked at me sideways through squinted eyes and eventually said, "I thought I told you not to go back into that storage unit."

I lowered my head apologetically but looked up at him shrewdly. "I really couldn't help myself, Judge—it was gut instinct…"

Chapter 55

Miller drove two and a half hours to the Greenhaven Correctional Facility to pay Warren Roller a visit. Mr. Roller's jury trial had been swift, being charged and convicted of armed robbery based on the security-camera evidence, as well as second-degree murder in the fatal shooting of Gina Modigliani. Mr. Roller would be spending a long, long time behind bars.

Warren Roller did not appear to be the brightest of men. His appearance was actually caveman-like, his eyes red, dull and lifeless. He was led into the visitor's room in wrist and ankle bracelets that accessorized the Halloween-orange jumpsuit quite nicely. Even after he came to rest in his chair, his cuffs continued to rattle from delirium tremens.

Miller questioned him about the day of his arrest. "What ever possessed you to go back to the crime scene?"

"The Big M Bakery, man. They make the best fuckin' cannoli around."

"If you valued their product so much, why would you want to rob them in the first place?"

"Hey, man—give me a break. I needed more crank, all right? That bakery has customers comin' and goin' all day. They make a ton of dough in there. Heh, heh—get it? Dough?"

Miller groaned and glared at him.

"I just thought they had plenty to share with the community—know what I'm sayin'?"

"So, you didn't hear on the news that they had captured your mug on camera?"

"I forgot, man—all right? My brain is pretty fried—know what I'm sayin'?"

"On the day of your arrest, you spoke directly to someone who was in the store—Rena Lorence. Did you know her?"

"Yeah—I knew Rena. We went to school together. I don't think she recognized me, though. It's gotta be at least twenty years since I last saw her. I used to be real fat. Most of the kids made fun—they called me 'Tuh-tuh-tootsie Roll.' But not Rena, though, man. She was one good egg. I finally lost all the weight when I got hooked on the lid poppers—know what I'm sayin'?"

Miller wondered why all prisoners used that phrase. He was also aghast that Roller knew me. Miller decided there really could be no connection between Roller and my catching the last bus out of town. He was too much of a nincompoop to think of anything *that* diabolical.

Miller drove back north on the Thruway, compiling all of the information he had so far and trying to dissect each fact further. As he rehashed his conversation with Roller, he couldn't help laugh out loud at the inanity of the now slim "Tootsie Roll" going back to the scene of the crime for, as he put it "the best fuckin' cannoli around"—what a pip...

Chapter 56

Though Lulu was deaf, she most assuredly could feel vibrations. Judge and I worked out a new musical arrangement for her so she'd be able to join in on the festivities once again. Judge purchased a couple of amplifiers and placed them face down on the ground on either side of the paddock gate. We recruited Lady Buggé to stomp and dance by Lulu, then slowly polka her way back toward Judge—who did play a mean accordion, I will admit. Today, Lady Buggé was wearing a lovely flowery, rose-pink, georgette dress with white high-top sneakers and a New York Yankee's baseball cap. At least the bill was facing forward. She took this new dance ritual quite seriously, with the expectation that Lulu would begin producing milk. I joined her on my last day of treatment and actually got her to crack a smile as we clapped and two-stepped, fitting in an occasional do-si-do. When Judge stopped playing, Lady Buggé never noticed. As we walked up the hill toward the house, she remained all a-twirl, apparently still feeling the beat. Lulu and Yosef were on their backs in the dirt, rocking and kicking which, from a distance, looked like they were in hysterical laughter. Where's the camera when you need it.

Judge started a pot of brew and I settled in at the kitchen nook where the view of the corral was perfect. I amused myself for a few minutes more while he got us set up with cups, spoons, sugar and cream.

"Well, Judge? What's the word?"

"Police searched Walway's apartment and storage unit yesterday afternoon, confiscating all of his videos, clothing, sheets, towels and even his mattress. There was definitely blood evidence. Walway was nowhere to be found but an APB has been issued. Ms. Williams provided her sister's hair and toothbrushes for DNA comparisons. We should know more later today. I'm sure there will be something on the six o'clock news tonight."

My heart thumping was so fierce I could feel my torso rock. My hands looked like I had just let go of a jackhammer. I couldn't believe I was reacting so intensely to the news—so much for being amused.

"I wonder if he's at his mother's," I thought aloud.

"There were no address books anywhere at his place and the visiting nurses said he had listed Sandy Williams as his emergency contact—no mother noted."

"He must have been watching her, then, even before the visiting nurses started services," I said.

"Watching?" Judge posed. "Try stalking. Sophie informed investigators of Sandy's past three employers prior to CVS—a bookstore near SUNY Binghamton, a café in Saratoga and a market in Albany. Security-camera tapes at each place during the term of her employment showed Ralph Walway videotaping her as she worked. The SUNY tape was the only one where he was not in a wheelchair. This all took place over the past five years."

"Was there anyone with him—a woman—someone helping him?"

"There was a woman with him but only in the CVS security tape. They are going to see if the visiting nurses can ID the woman as one of their home health aides."

"Poor woman is probably dead."

Judge flipped on the small kitchen TV for news at noon. Top story showed a picture of Ralph's boyish face across the screen. The din sounding in my ears was like being in a roomful of cicadas. I felt like I might pass out, but then they flashed a picture of Sandy Williams and everything stopped—the noise in my head, the nervous hands. My senses were at heightened alert. The reporter was saying that Ralph Walway was wanted for questioning in the woman's disappearance and that further investigations were pending. My hands resumed a slower rhythm as I tried to put a spoonful of sugar in my coffee cup. The bowl toppled and Judge McG. helped me scrape up the crystals as best we could for the moment, leaving a pattern of fine lines on the glass tabletop.

Judge looked worriedly at me but said with a soothing confidence, "We'll find him, you know."

Lady Buggé opened the screen door with drama, patting the perspiration off her face and neck with a lace handkerchief. She looked thoroughly satisfied after her day's work. She had taken off her high-tops at some point during her earlier revue and they now dangled from two fingers. I could only hope that what was squished between her toes was, indeed, mud.

"I need a cosmo," she sighed. She walked over to where we sat, stared a moment at the table and then curiously at me, saying "My, my, sweetie—you look jittery." She wet a fingertip and blotted some of the scraped-up lines of sugar, dabbing it on the end of her tongue and across her gums with narc-like expertise. "You know, dear—this stuff will do it to you every time..."

Chapter 57

"Well, Miller, honey—I tried, but I couldn't come up with anything poison related." Elisha and Miller met at the same diner as before. "But I *did* find some very unusual magazines and news articles, plus a *slew* of prescription medicines that were lying around. I wrote it all down like you told me." Elisha handed Miller a folder.

"Wow, Elisha—this is quite organized. Great job. You didn't touch anything in his room, did you?"

"What—you think I'm a rookie?" She giggled playfully like a schoolgirl. "I wore those disposable surgical gloves as I always do when I'm collecting trash. I don't think you'd find one of my prints in *any* of the rooms."

Miller smiled. He took out the contents of the folder and scanned the first page. It was a list of magazines:
- *Back Stage*
- *Rolling Stone*
- *Stage and Screen*
- *Hollywood Reporter*

- *People*
- *LA Times*

"Huh," Miller grunted. "This guy is really into celebrities and entertainment." Miller flipped to the next page, which was a list of medications:
- Oxycontin (pain reliever)
- Tylenol 3 (pain reliever)
- Hydrocodone (pain reliever)
- Flexeril (muscle relaxant)
- Zoloft (anti-depressant)
- Ambien (sedative)

"Like I said before, Miller—this guy has about as much pain as I do beauty."

"Well, Elisha—beauty *is* in the eye of the beholder, in case you haven't heard," Miller teased.

"Oh, you. Anyway, this guy is just a big dope addict—no doubt about it," Elisha said definitively.

The last page was headed "Miscellaneous." Elisha explained, "I just went through his room randomly and wrote down a few items I felt were of note." The first item—possibly a screenplay or movie script. "The first several pages were folded over and I couldn't see a title or author, but I thought it strange that he'd be reading a movie script though it certainly does coincide with his choice of magazines."

Miller added, "This would also go along with your hypothesis that the guy *is* an actor and would explain how he so easily got away with lying to his wife and employer."

The second item—plain business envelope with "one-half" written on the front of it.

"What's with the envelope?" Miller looked at Elisha warily, hoping she had a good explanation.

"That, my dear, really caught my eye because it was next to the script and there was money sticking out of it. There was no address for Gus on it or a return address so it must have been delivered by hand. I didn't touch it in case he had the money set up a certain way and was testing the staff. I did question the rest of the staff to see if Gus had any recent visitors, but they all said they hadn't seen anyone come in. It could be partial payment up front for a part he's going to play. Who knows, but everyone agrees that Gus has not been around much these days and they all think he's trying to avoid chores. He hasn't volunteered for anything at the shelter and he uses his pain as an excuse. Well—no one I've ever known in *that* much pain could be out and about all day long like he is."

"I am truly impressed, Elisha. I think, though, that if the money was for a part in a play or movie, it would be dealt with much more professionally, like through a contract and a bank check."

Miller continued with his inspection of Elisha's findings. The third item—obit on night stand for Corinne Davison—died suddenly April 1, 2002.

"His sister," Miller blurted.

"Gus had a sister?"

"Yes—he told me that the day of Rena's death."

"Did he tell you she died on April Fool's Day?"

"No—but if I remember correctly, he said he hadn't seen or spoken with her in a few years."

"Well—I guess there's a good reason for that, now, isn't there? I didn't see Gus's name listed as a survivor, though. Then again, I was reading it upside down and trying to hurry."

The last item—envelope from Virgin Airlines—tickets to London Heathrow—May 21st departure. "I couldn't resist looking at this one," Elisha said, her eyes sparkling like fairy dust. "This guy is bookin' out of here in *three days!* Just thought you'd be interested in knowing that little tidbit. So, Miller—there you have it. I've dissected his life as best I could without getting caught or even raising suspicion."

"You are one super duper private eye, Elisha," Miller said proudly. "I just wish I could somehow relate your findings to Rena's death. Gus suddenly leaving town, though, just might be newsworthy…"

Chapter 58

I had cancelled the rest of my patients after my visit with Judge. Seeing that first news report had really thrown me for a loop. Ed and I hadn't had dinner together at a decent hour in such a long time, so it was nice to be able to get home early and cook Ed his favorite—broiled salmon. We settled close together to catch the six o'clock news. Moose sat next to me, butt on the couch, front feet on the floor, as eager to hear the latest as we were. Maggie had just gotten tossed outside after getting caught on the kitchen counter eating our leftover salmon. The local anchor started with "Breaking News" and I squeezed the top of Ed's knee. *"Stop it! That tickles!"*

Ralph Walway was shown being led in handcuffs by local police, "arrested earlier this afternoon on insurance fraud charges and suspicion of stalking, assault and kidnapping in relation to a recently reported missing persons' case involving Sandy Williams. A full-blown search and investigation is underway to find this young woman from Latham. There may be other local missing women who were once associated with Mr. Walway. No further details were made available by police." Ralph's head was lowered hard in an attempt to conceal his face, but his full mug shot was shown in the split-screen depiction above Sandy's photo. Ralph's court-appointed defense attorney had "no comment" for press, but it was further reported that Mr. Walway had planned to hire one of the best criminal defense attorneys in the country. Moose's head tilted side to side as he watched Ralph being escorted away and, at one point, uttered a low growl.

"Wow," Ed said. "Guess he knows a bad guy when he sees one."

"Yeah—the growling toward Ralph started the day he hit me in the head with the storage door. Moose was clearly meant to be with me from that point on," I said, as I patted his big ol' rump. Moose turned to look at me with droopy lower lids and flopped on my arm what I considered to be the longest tongue I had ever seen, just letting it rest there as if to savor our friendship.

"I wonder if they'll ever find her," I said, as Ed pulled me closer. "Poor Sophie—I just can't fathom what she was feeling when she saw that video of her sister. Half of my soul would die if I ever saw Lydia being tortured like that."

"What about this guy's mother? Didn't you say he always went to visit her during your treatments?"

"You know, Ed, I really wonder now if there is a 'mother.' I mean everyone has a mother, but I'm thinking now that scenario was just a ruse."

"Well, I'm sure we'll find out soon enough…"

Chapter 59

Ralph Walway had hired Otis Elis for his defense. Otis, "My'Man," as all his well-heeled clients referred to him, had a one hundred percent success rate. He could raise reasonable doubt even if the perp was caught at the scene, weapon (or dick—depending on the crime) in hand. And, if it were a woman—well, let's not go there. *DNA?* Didn't matter. Mr. Elis always found a snag in the case to get his client off. Ralph's appearance the day of his arraignment was quite natty. He was dressed in a conservative, navy-blue suit, white shirt and a plain, red silk tie—right, Mr. All American. My'Man, however, was quite the opposite. Always the showboat, he donned a deep-purple silk suit, black shirt and a tie depicting the crucifixion of Jesus Christ. Ralph had the nerve to walk into the courtroom that day with the assist of Canadian crutches, taking the bulk of his weight on his arms and swinging both legs forward in unison.

The presiding Judge, Rathbone Hillcott, just stared at the defendant and his counsel, as DA Knower recited the charges raised by "The People."

"*Mr.* Walway—how are you going to plead to these charges?"

Hillcott's voice was a baritone rumble of thunder.

Ralph, of course, pled innocent the day of his arraignment to charges of insurance fraud, stalking, assault and kidnapping. He had now spent six months in jail awaiting jury selection and a trial date, as Judge Hillcott set bail at an unaffordable amount. His jury (let's hope *not* of his peers) had just been selected and his trial now underway.

Prosecution called several witnesses, most of them associated with the visiting nurses—Ralph's nurse, physical and occupational therapists, social worker and mental health nurse, plus two of the home health aides. Ralph had a total of five aides over the short time he had received services but it turned out that three of the five, who allegedly quit, had subsequently been listed as "missing persons."

Each of the professionals testified to the fact that, in their collective opinion, Ralph was attempting to magnify the severity of his injuries in order to avoid work and remain on the State's dole. They all spoke of Ralph's obsession with keeping his bathroom off-limits. The two therapists testified that Ralph dismissed them after the first three weeks of services because, in his words, he could not gain anything more functionally. They also corroborated that, due to their specific testing for range of motion, muscle tone, functional abilities and obvious inconsistencies in his movements, Ralph was an exaggerating malingerer. One of the aides reported that she walked into his apartment one time and found Ralph standing at the refrigerator. He quickly hobbled back to his wheelchair, hanging on to whatever was available to get there, acting as if he had just run a marathon. The other aide said she had quit after her first week because Ralph was just too demanding, wanting her to do more than what was required on the care plan. Both aides said that something in their gut told them to get out and never look back. That, of course, was objected to and sustained. The social worker asserted that she had attempted to get Ralph employment assistance through the Department of Labor, but he refused. At her follow-up visit with Ralph, he presented a doctor's note, which stated Ralph was unable to return to work at that time. She had attempted to speak with Ralph's doctor on several occasions, always having to leave a message but never receiving a return phone call. The mental health nurse swore that Ralph laughed outright when she called for an appointment and he refused to even see her for an evaluation. He told her he was not crazy and didn't want to be labeled by some shrink.

Cross-examination was brief. Otis My'Man paraded flamboyantly in front of the jury with his duplicitous questioning and use of extravagant hand gestures. His attempts to trip up each one of them in one way or another succeeded. Ralph's nurse, Michelle, had said that when assessing his medication use, she discovered he wasn't taking any of the pain pills as ordered by the doctor yet he complained of pain at each of her visits. My'Man argued that his client was trying to stay alert and be as independent as possible. "Ralph didn't want to be dependent on drugs, which is a very good thing—right, Ms. Bingham?"

"Objection—leading the witness."

"Overruled—you may answer the question."

"Of course it's a good thing to not want to be drug-dependent, but keeping your pain levels controlled for greater function is even better. If his pain were better controlled, perhaps he *could* return to work. There are studies that confirm that people with chronic pain who use medication to control it will not develop an addiction to that substance."

Mr. Elis shot the jury a questionable look as if what Michelle had just said was absurd. "So now your expertise is greater than the attending physician. Do you have written proof of these studies with you today, Ms. Bingham?"

"Well, no—I don't—but…"

"No more questions, Your Honor."

To Kimberly Howell, the physical therapist, My'Man bombastically posed, "Isn't it true, Ms. P.T. Howell, that no two people respond to therapy in exactly the same way—meaning that the exact same injury sustained by two people, no matter how alike they may be, can have completely different results?"

"Objection—leading and I would say to the brink of badgering, Your Honor."

"Overruled—answer the question, young lady."

"Yes, of course that's true, but that analysis could apply to one person on any given day, for that matter. We all have our good and bad days and respond differently to injury, physical or mental, depending on how we're feeling at that particular time. My observations of…"

"I didn't ask for any more of your observations. No more questions."

To Minnie Thorpe, the occupational therapist, My'Man more politely offered, "Isn't it true that, even for the able-bodied, we could all work at the same job but in different capacities, with varying levels of endurance and with completely mixed outcomes?"

"Objection."

"What exactly are you objecting to, Mr. Knower?" Judge Hillcott asked with annoyance.

"Mr. Elis is going nowhere with his questioning. He's just rephrasing and I, as well as the jury—I'm sure—am getting bored with his histrionic oratory."

"Overruled, Mr. Knower. I, myself, am not bored. Kindly answer the question, Ms. Thorpe."

"Of course, that's true, but…"

"No more questions."

Jeannette Raymond, the social worker, simply stated she didn't agree with the doctor's assessment that Ralph was unable to work. She went on to quickly tell the jury that Ralph was able to drive, which gave him complete independence, and that he even assisted his ailing mother on a weekly basis. My'Man interrupted and ridiculed her for her attempt at comparing her master of social work degree to that of a medical doctor. "No more questions."

"Objection."

"Overruled."

"According to the visiting nurses 'Patient Bill of Rights,' a patient has the right to refuse any service offered—without question." My'Man was questioning Penny Piedmont, the mental health nurse.

"That's correct, b-but…"

"No more questions for this witness, Your Honor."

"Objection! She was not done answering the question."

"Overruled. She answered Mr. Elis' question. You may step down, Ms. Piedmont."

My'Man made mincemeat out of the two home health aides, lobbing one question after another down their throats, tripping them up and diminishing their characters based on lack of education and experience. They both became quite emotional and flustered, giving conflicting testimony. His projectile method of catechizing was spliced by snippets of tossed-out objections.

Mr. Elis kept witnesses for Ralph's defense at a minimum. They included a hooker who had been a longtime acquaintance of Ralph's, his primary physician and a high school friend. The hooker, who had starred in a few of Ralph's movies, said, "So Ralph's not paralyzed—big whoop-ti-do—but he's no kidnapper or killer. He's just into some innocent S&M." She admitted to DA Knower that Ralph got a little rough at times, but she felt that was all part of the show. She also said she didn't know she was being filmed but knowing that now was a "turn-on." She concurred with the others that Ralph would not let *her* use the bathroom in his apartment either, which she did think was pretty weird, but her visits with Ralph "didn't last long," which resulted in a good deal of snickering throughout the courtroom.

Ralph's primary physician, Dr. Drew Shade, brought Ralph's initial x-rays and MRI results to show that his injuries were very real, which were entered into evidence. He testified that he was aware Ralph was trying very hard not to take an excessive amount of pain medication. He also reported that Ralph was suffering from posttraumatic stress and that he was personally providing counseling for Ralph. He felt Ralph was far from ready to be working, stating that Ralph had suffered enough without having to go through additional stress, like this trial. He admitted to DA Knower that the VNA staff had reported their findings of what they felt were Ralph's exaggerations of his injuries and decreased overall physical abilities. However, he didn't necessarily believe in these modern-day therapies and, therefore, took everything they had to say with not just a grain but a shaker of salt. He didn't have any objection to Ralph's dismissing them. When asked why he ordered their services through the home-care agency in the first place, he replied, "I didn't want Ralph to feel he was being deprived of any service available out there. It was his decision to accept or reject them."

Ralph's high school friend painted a Dali-esque angelic picture of

Ralph, dripping with surrealism, and it was obvious the jury was keeping an intuitive, collective eye on both of them.

DA Knower recalled the physical therapist for re-direct, reminding her she was still under oath. He went on to explain to Judge Hillcott and the jury that since Ms. Howell had more to say on cross about her observations of Mr. Walway but was not allowed, he now wanted to give her that opportunity. He asked, "Ms. Howell, is it unusual for a paraplegic to be able to use crutches as Mr. Walway has demonstrated his ability to do so here today?"

"No, it is not unusual. With normal or better upper body strength and the use of momentum, crutches are a common assistive device used for ambulation."

"The People ask this court's permission for Mr. Walway to demonstrate his ability to ambulate from the defense table to the jury box and back, Your Honor."

"Objection, Judge Hillcott. That is an outrageous request to ask that we put Mr. Walway and his spinal cord injury on display. That would just be adding insult to injury."

"Overruled, Mr. Elis. This court finds the People's request reasonable. Mr. Walway, kindly oblige Mr. Knower by walking to the jury box and then return to your seat. Mr. Knower, please accompany Mr. Walway in the event he requires assistance."

Ralph awkwardly pushed himself to upright with the use of his crutches, adjusting the arm cuffs over his suit jacket. He began ambulating with DA Knower by his side. As Ralph turned and started back toward his seat, the DA said, "Ms. Howell—please—a gait evaluation."

"For one thing, Mr. Walway is using his hip flexor and abdominal muscles to swing his legs forward, knee flexion and ankle dorsiflexion to keep his legs from dragging on the floor."

Ralph halted momentarily and then attempted to finish the trek back to his table with flourish. DA Knower then turned to observe the jury's reaction. The majority appeared to acknowledge the discrepancies as Ralph plopped himself back in his seat.

"Continue, Ms. Howell."

"Even with Mr. Walway's incomplete spinal cord lesion at the mid- to lower-thoracic level as reported by Dr. Shade, it is highly unlikely that he would be able to prevent his feet from dragging on the floor without the use of orthotics, at least for supporting the ankles. He would also require the orthotic to extend to the knees in order to be able to weightbear as Mr. Walway did when he first stood."

"Thank you, Ms. Howell, for that astute observation. With the court's permission, we would request that Mr. Walway show the jury his lower-extremity orthotics."

"Objection! Mr. Knower is making a mockery of my client and this court proceeding, Your Honor."

"Overruled, Mr. Elis. I will allow all further questioning along these lines. Please proceed."

DA Knower, with those grizzly-bear paws, pushed Ralph's chair out in the open where the jury could freely observe. "Mr. Walway, kindly show the jury the orthotics you wear to aid in your ambulation."

Ralph's face glowed with humiliation and anger. "I'm not wearing any. I am able to periodically lift my feet and tighten my knee muscles because my spinal cord injury was incomplete." There was a reverberating murmur throughout the courtroom.

"Ms. Howell—is there anything else you would like to add at this time?"

"I would—thank you. According to the initial test results Dr. Shade presented, the stated impression of the radiologist at the bottom of those films indicated edema. There was no mention of a lesion or laceration. I'm wondering how Dr. Shade came to that conclusion in his final diagnosis."

"Objection, Your Honor! This so-called therapist does not have the education to make a medical diagnosis. Ms. Howell does not know what she is talking about."

"Overruled for the last time, Mr. Elis. Please continue."

DA Knower was looking almost smug. "Ms. Howell? Kindly state the extent of your education for the jury."

"Happily. I have a master's of science in physical therapy, a Ph.D. in spinal cord injuries, a Ph.D. in neuropathology, a Ph.D. in neuropsychiatry and a Ph.C., which is a degree in pharmaceutical chemistry. On that note, I would like to go on record that I concur with Ms. Bingham's testimony of non-addiction to analgesics and narcotics in the presence of true pain."

"My, my, Ms. Howell. How many years of higher education does that total?"

"Twenty four—I guess you could say I like being a student."

"Thank you, Ms. Howell. Your Honor, I'd like to re-call Dr. Shade to the stand."

Dr. Shade fidgeted with his tie as he once again sat in the hot seat.

"You're a general practioner, correct?"

"Yes, that's right."

"How many years of medical school have you had, sir?"

Mr. Elis whipped out of his seat like batter from a bowl but before he could open his mouth, Judge Hillcott roared, "Sit down, Mr. Elis, or you will be in contempt." My'Man promptly sunk back in his seat like a failed soufflé.

"Twelve."

"Hmm—half the time Ms. Howell has specialized in spinal cord injuries and neuroscience. No more questions, Your Honor."

DA Knower then introduced and presented over a five-day period the videos found in Ralph's apartment. He saved the worst for last. The films showed there were several other women being whipped, pummeled and otherwise tortured. His moods were like Mt. St. Helens, spewing pent-up hatred, waiting for just the right moment—or woman—to fully erupt. That hapless, helpless woman was Sandy Williams. Watching that fateful footage, the courtroom was generally lulled, mouths agape, though one could hear an occasional gasp from both spectators and jury members. Whispers of words such as "audacious" and "detestable" could be heard. Newspaper reports, over the course of the next few days, added "virulant" and "scabrous" to the list. Sick jokes flew from mouth to ear, like a child's game of tea table gossip. "Hey—what do you call it when a right turn leads to a dead end? What? A Ralph Wrongway." Soon after, Ralph was referred to as "Wrongway Walway."

Sophie Williams was the final witness called by prosecution to testify about her missing sister. She identified her as being the woman beaten by Ralph in the last film shown and that Sandy had been missing since around the time immediately before Ralph's arrest. Sophie tried to remain composed but when Sandy's answering machine tape of Ralph's message was played for the jury, she lost it. She glared through a blur of tears at Ralph and choked, "You fucking bastard! You killed her! What did you do with her? Where is she?"

Otis My'Man objected profusely and Judge Hillcott called for order as the courtroom spectators became ingredients in the roiled pot of mixed emotions.

After a short recess, DA Knower made a request to enter taped testimony. "Your Honor, this witness was Rena Lorence. You may have seen her name mentioned in the papers. She died recently as a result of foul play."

"Objection! Irrelevant to this case. I do declare, Your Honor."

"Overruled, Mr. Elis," Judge Hillcott's voice clapped. "I find it quite interesting that Ms. Lorence's homicide *co*-incides with the beginning of this trial. Your client might just get witness tampering added to his list of charges. As I'm sure you are well aware, taped testimony can be presented if a witness is no longer able to appear and, I assure you, this witness is unable to appear at this time. Agreed?" That final word rolled off his tongue now at bass level.

My taped testimony was allowed and presented. It was the grand overture and finale all at once. Ralph was visibly shaken. He was scribbling notes furiously to My'Man.

"Objection, Your Honor! That woman invaded Mr. Walway's right to privacy, after he specifically asked her not to enter that room." Ralph scribbled another quick note. "Plus, Judge Hillcott—*Your Honor*—there is no evidence, based on all the tapes that were shown in this court, that Ms. Lorence or anyone else ever entered that room."

"Overruled, Mr. Elis. Please sit down and allow Mr. Knower to present the rest of his case. "

DA Knower then showed the tape that I had interrupted that final day. There I was, working with Moose on the bed, looking casually around the room, emoting in an obviously louder tone and enunciating my words carefully as I told Moose I was going to the lobby to use the bathroom. Then snow and static for five minutes before recording resumed and the room was empty. The only difference was that I had left the bathroom door wide open in my rush to get the hell out of there.

DA Knower then called forensics to the stand to testify about the blood DNA comparisons and matches found in the bathroom and on Ralph's mattress.

My'Man lowered and shook his head. He whispered in Ralph's ear for a moment and asked for a recess.

"Five minutes—that's it," Judge Hillcott ordered.

DA Knower waited outside the courtroom. Judge McGillacuddy approached him. "I've been following the case. You're doing a top-notch job. There's no way Elis will win this one."

"Let's hope not. That tie My'Man wore to the arraignment was prophetic."

When everyone returned to the courtroom, Otis Elis conceded that substantial evidence had been shown to convict Mr. Walway on the fraud charge. He stated that, based on all of the publicity the case was getting, Mr. Walway was willing to change his plea to guilty in the fraud charge only and be willing to bargain. DA Knower rejected the plea. After a magniloquent closing by My'Man and with DA Knower simply reiterating the facts, the jury convened. Deliberations were the shortest in DA Knower's history of prosecutions. Within twenty minutes, they returned with findings of guilty on charges of insurance fraud, stalking and assault. Judge Hillcott then took the opportunity and great pleasure in excoriating Ralph.

"Ralph Walway, based on the footage I've witnessed here today and all of the testimony put before me, you will be remanded to a state correctional facility with sentencing to be decided two weeks from today. Now, Mr. Elis, I suggest you hold your tongue while I expound my revulsion to your client. One word from you and you *will* be held in contempt." Judge Hillcott paused briefly to inhale and keep control of his own contempt, then took aim. "You, Mr. Walway, are lower than vermin. You are akin to a communicable disease—a syphilis on our souls—an abhorrent, slithering behemoth with a nefarious appetite for the dear mim women on this earth. You are loathsome and horrid—an inky harbinger of doom. You are fallacious, eely and stinking up my courtroom. Realize that investigations are ongoing for the suspicion of your involvement in kidnapping and murder…"

Chapter 60

There was just no way I was going to the Derrow residence again unless that dog was there. I punched in their phone number and decided I would hang up after five rings. Selma answered on the fourth. She sounded shaken.

"Selma—it's Rena. What's wrong?"

"Oh, Rena, dear," she said in a croak. "Bernard died." She excused herself a moment and I could hear that she was dabbing away her sorrow.

"Selma—I'm so sorry. What happened?"

"Dr. Roberts said that Bernard developed an infection. They thought they had everything under control with his medications but found him dead yesterday morning. He died of renal failure. We picked up his body immediately and decided to bury him in my flower garden. Some wild animal must have picked up on the scent and made a huge mess during the night trying to dig him up. Armando was so upset this morning over the disturbance that he voiced his frustration with Louis, who then fired him—on the spot! Then Alena quit! I am so distraught, Rena. I'm just beside myself!"

"My God, Selma—I can't believe it. Armando and Alena did *everything* for you."

"I know, Rena. Louis is out of control. He's really losing it. Do you think you can come by to see me in a couple of days? I'll still pay you. I'm desperate for someone to talk to, Rena."

"I'll call you, Selma. Maybe instead of your place we could meet somewhere for lunch. I really couldn't handle another scene with Louis."

"That's fine, dear. It'll be my treat. Plus, I'll pay you for the time and trouble from our last visit. See you then."

This had been my first conversation with Selma where she mentioned their vet's name. I don't know why I had never asked her for it. I combed the yellow pages and found a Richard Roberts on Route 30 in Middleburgh. I thought I should at least talk with the DVM in charge so I'd have a scrap of communication to justify my being paid for services in this case, or lack thereof.

"Dr. Roberts—may I help you?"

"Yes—my name is Rena Lorence. I'm an animal therapist who was hired by Selma Derrow. She told me today that your office was treating her poodle, Bernard, and that he died this week. I was just calling to confirm the cause of death. I don't think Mrs. Derrow completely understood in her grief."

"I know of Mrs. Derrow, but she hasn't had any pets in here for at least five years."

"Okay—now I'm confused. Did I hear you right? Could I possibly have the wrong office? Is there another vet by the name of Roberts in this area?"

"Yes, you heard right and, no, I'm the only vet by the name of Roberts around these parts."

I was starting to feel lightheaded, so I thanked him and hung up. I was totally muddled—no, sad—no, outraged. I was going to call Selma and ream her out. On second thought, I'd meet her as agreed, get paid, have a free lunch and then confront her. On my way, I would stop at Wellington's Herbs for a calming blend of tea.

She met me at the Alley Cat diner in Schoharie two days later. She was her cool, elegant self and had tried desperately to conceal the check-on luggage that hung blatantly under her eyes. She handed me another container of baked yummies. We ordered, chitchatted and ate, without bringing up any of the dog business, which was pretty strange for someone who just lost their only pet. The waitress brought the tab and Selma reached for it. "My treat—remember?" She coolly opened her purse and reached in. She removed her hand and looked at me with surprise. "I forgot my wallet. I'm so embarrassed. I promise I'll reimburse you."

I handed the waitress my Visa and looked at Selma with one eyebrow arched. "I placed a call to Dr. Roberts the other day. He seemed a bit confused. He said you hadn't been in his office with a pet for at least five years. Why, Selma—why would you ever make up such a lie? Are you *that* desperate for friendship?"

Selma's posture stiffened. Her chin lifted and shifted in marionette-like fashion. She was silent. She knew she had no recourse for her bullshit any more than I for my services.

"You know, Selma—I really do feel for you. You obviously have more than your share of problems. You've tried to either ignore or hide Louis' illness and because of that you've lost the only two people who had devoted nearly ten years of their lives to helping you. Plus I'm positive that *you* were the only reason they stayed on for as long as they did. Then you deceive me and have now lost my friendship. Why in the world did you ever hire me in the first place?"

"I don't know, Rena. I heard of your services and just thought it was a good way to meet someone new—an animal lover—someone with something in common with me. I just needed another person to talk to."

"It sounds like you just needed someone *new* to talk to, Selma. Everyone else was fed up with Louis' bloated ego, his capricious mood and his pickled brain, not to mention your coddling, haughty ignorance and sniveling. You wasted my time and, besides that, I have a feeling I'm not going to see a dime for my last visit and my time frittered away here today."

Selma tried but was unable to hold my tenacious glare. Her chin still raised, she stared out the diner window and remained silent.

As I stood to leave, I leaned over the table and whispered, "You're sick, Selma. You need help. You might want to consider seeking counsel—both mental and legal…"

Chapter 61

When Miller arrived, Judge McG. was playing a rousing tune for the increased herd of animals he had acquired. Miller sauntered toward the corral smiling as he caught sight of Lady Buggé hoofin' it—so to speak—among the llamas, goats and a gorgeous Morgan mare. It was a bizarre but somehow pleasing scene. Judge McG. had been expecting him. He stopped playing but, as usual, Lady Buggé continued dancing.

"That's quite a gig you've got there," Miller said, as they started toward the house.

"The best audience around. You must be Miller Sampson," Judge said as he extended his hand. "Call me Franklin."

"So, Judge—Franklin—when Rena was visiting here, did she treat *all* of these animals?"

"Oh, no—I only had the two llamas then. Rena was the one who figured out my new setup with the amps, though, to engage my deaf girl, Lulu."

"Oh, so *that's* why she was still dancing."

Judge laughed. "No, no—my wife Marylou isn't deaf. She just doesn't *want* to stop dancing. I was referring to one of my llamas. The other animals came after Rena was done with her sessions. I got the goats for milk because Marylou was dead set on having fresh milk every morning. Unfortunately, the llamas weren't cooperating."

They both chuckled.

"My horse, Clementine, came last. I just thought it would be fun to be able to ride again—hadn't saddled up since I was a kid. She's a gentle, ol' girl." Judge looked pensive for a moment. "Well, now—what can I do for you?"

"I understand you and Rena had become pretty good friends during her time here. I heard you helped her with putting Ralph Walway behind bars."

"Yes, Miller—that's right—though I think Rena really didn't need my help. She had the wherewithal and the balls—pardon the vernacular—to do it all on her own. I was just able to speed up the investigation a tad."

"Did she ever speak with you about any of her other clients?"

"Oh, you bet. She met quite an array of personalities in her field."

Miller showed Judge McG. the list of clients he had already questioned. "Can you think of anyone else I may have missed?"

Judge took a moment to scan the list and the recesses of his brain. "There is one person I remember who's not on this list. Her name was Selma. I remember it because of the character on the old show *Night Court*. Sorry to say I don't know her last name, though—don't think Rena ever mentioned it. From what I recall, Rena was furious with her because the woman pretended to have a dog that needed services, but Rena found out eventually that there was no dog. I remember Rena saying something about the woman's husband—I think his name was Louis—being alcoholic. She also said how much she really hated that whole scene."

"Was the last name 'Bernard' by any chance?"

"No—but I do think that was the name the woman used for her non-existent dog. When Rena found out that she had been lured into this woman's horrible life with her barbless line of lies, she confronted her and advised her to get help. From my recollection, that was the last time Rena had any contact with the woman."

"Do you know about how long ago this happened, Judge?"

"Well—let's see. It seems it was some time after the arrest of Ralph Walway—so maybe a couple of months ago now?"

"That's great information, Judge. You've been more than helpful. I think I'll run a second check on all phone calls made from the Lorence residence and Rena's cell phone. I just don't recall their names being on our original phone list. We've investigated contacts over the past six months even though the level of chemicals in her system could only have been introduced over a two- to three-month time frame."

"Rena may have made her calls from someone else's home. She used our phone a few times to call other clients."

"Judge, you may have just opened up the biggest lead in this case."

"We can only hope, Miller. Rena didn't deserve this—no one does, for that matter. Good luck with the case and let me know if I can help you out with anything else."

"Appreciate it, Judge, though I'm getting the feeling that there's something truly fishy about this Selma character…"

Chapter 62

"I doan know, Arrrmando—I think something bad is going on over therre."

"Alena—the only thing bad is that we were fired. I should sue that son of a bitch for wrongful termination. But—before I do that—I need to go back over there to gather up my tools before Louis comes up with some flimsy excuse to keep them."

"I'll come with you. I also left some things in the house. I must tell you, Arrrmando—I'm worried about the mizzuz. I hope she is all rrright."

When Armando and Alena arrived at the Derrow residence, they went to the back door, as was their usual and required by Louis. Selma was in the back yard instructing a young man at the far end of the garden. Armando leaned toward Alena's ear. "Look—she's already hired my replacement." He spit with disgust on the walkway.

"Stop that, Arrrmando!"

Selma heard their voices and acknowledged them with a wave, primly making her way across the rain-soaked lawn.

"Mizzuz D.—I need to pick up my cleaning supplies and Arrrmando needs to get his tools."

"Oh, Alena—do come in for a minute. I miss you terribly."

"*No*," Armando said quickly. "We will wait outside."

Alena handed Selma a list of things to pack together and said she would wait with Armando.

The new gardener had gone to the tool shed as they waited. Armando slowly headed toward the garden where the man had been working.

"Arrrmando—wherre do you think you arre going?"

"I want to see what kind of shit work this poor slob has done. I'll get my tools in a minute before the bastard gets too comfortable with them."

"Oh, Arrrmando!" Alena said as she threw her hands up in the air but then decided to follow closely behind him. They both witnessed the new gardener quickly leave the tool shed and exit the gate on the opposite side of the house. They just stared at one another as they heard a vehicle start and pull away.

"Wow—that was verrry strrange."

"If he took any of my tools, I'll sue them for that as well."

They reached the edge of the flower bed where it merged with a hedgerow of flowering shrubs.

"Look at this mess!" Armando squatted and then turned to face Alena with a look of disgust. "Do you smell that, Alena?"

Alena leaned closer to the soil. "Oh, my God—what *is* that, Arrrmando?"

"I don't really know, but I know it's not good."

Selma called from the back door and Alena joined her while Armando went to gather his tools. Selma appeared to be very nervous and Alena was shocked to see she was actually perspiring.

"Mizzuz D.—arre you okay?"

"Oh, dear Alena, I'm fine—not to worry. I was just trying to get your things together without disturbing Louis. I don't want him to give either of you any more trouble."

Armando was walking toward them with an overflow of gardening necessities in his arms. "Come now, Alena. We don't want to be late for our appointment." Alena scowled at him for the lie but understood his urgency to leave.

Driving away, Armando looked worried. "Alena—something is

seriously wrong at that place."

"I know, Arrrmando—Selma was sweating, forr Chrrist sakes!"

"I think we need to report our suspicions."

"Oh, what—go to the police and say 'we were firred frrom our jobs as garrdener and maid and now Selma is *sweating*?'"

"Well, when you put it that way it means nothing, but what about the putrid smell and the mysterious gardener?"

"He was jus' afrraid of you. But, that smell, Arrrmando—was that the smell of death?"...

Chapter 63

Miller was beginning to appreciate the gargoyle knocker and the people who lived behind it. Though Tiarra had been rather obtuse at the start of their relationship, Miller had come to appreciate her emerging self-confidence. And Chris—whoever and whatever—was a genuinely pleasant person to be around.

Chris opened the door and startled Miller from his private thoughts. "Miller! Come in, come in—the 'T' Lady is expecting you. She has a few things to tell you," Chris said teasingly. Miller smiled and entered. Tiarra came out of the kitchen, pushing a teacart loaded with goodies.

"I've got so much to tell you, Miller," she said excitedly, as she pushed the cart into the living room.

"So I've heard," Miller replied.

"I already warned him," Chris piped in with a smile.

"Well?" Miller helped himself to tea and cookies as Tiarra got herself settled in her easy-lift chair.

"Miller—I am convinced more than ever that a woman killed Rena. I have had the *strangest* visions."

"Go on."

"I was looking out my window a couple of days ago when I noticed a woman, standing in the middle of the road, staring at my house and crying. I stepped out on the porch to see if I could help her, but she slowly backed away, her head hung low, whispering, 'I'm sorry—I'm so, so sorry.' Then she vanished. I had thought she was a real woman, Miller, but then I realized it was the same voice I heard before. Then, yesterday, I opened the door to get the morning paper and she was right there on the porch, Miller! Her hand was on the doorknob! Again, she was crying and apologizing. When I reached for her, she was gone."

"Have you seen her yet today?" Miller asked

"No—I've been a little hesitant about opening my door—crazy, huh? Thought I'd just wait until you got here."

"Well—I'm ready—are you?"

Tiarra took a deep breath and said, "Let's go."

"I'll just wait in here, if you don't mind," Chris said with a blush of nervousness.

Miller took Tiarra by the arm and escorted her out on to her front porch. Tiarra's focus led Miller's eyes across the street. There was another funeral underway. Tiarra's body suddenly stiffened, almost in a seizure. Then she went limp and Miller had to ease her down into a chair.

'Déjà vu,' he mused. "What is it, Tiarra?"

"Give me a moment," she panted.

Miller fanned her face while she recovered.

"Over there—she's over there," Tiarra said sounding exhausted.

"Over where? Who is over where?"

"Let's wait until they leave."

"Until who leaves?"

"The people at that funeral. It's her, Miller—it's her funeral."

"Jesus!" He looked across where the funeral rite was just ending and felt both sadness and exhilaration. He wanted so much to rush over there and question everyone present, but that was obviously out of the question. It took another ten minutes or so before all of those dear had departed. Miller looked at Tiarra, who had been sitting with her head lowered and eyes closed. "Are you ready?"

"Hold on to me, Miller. My legs are like rubber."

They crossed the street and meandered through the necropolis in a tiptoe. When they reached the newly dug site, Miller was taken off guard. There, on the head stone, was the name Selma—Selma Derrow. Could it actually be *the* Selma?

"This is the woman—she knew Rena," Tiarra mourned.

Miller wrote down the name, plus the dates of her birth and death. He quietly led Tiarra back to her home and got her settled inside.

"Now I have a name, Tiarra, which means another lead, and I think this is going to be the one to settle the case and let Rena rest in peace."

Tiarra, in a sad voice but with conviction, said, "That's all we can ask for—rest in peace—dead or alive. It's any person's given right…"

Chapter 64

With DA Knower's aid in and practice at working out all the kinks, he was ready for my deposition.

"Does this mean I won't have to appear in court for trial?"

"Sorry, Rena—you'll still be subpoenaed to appear. Under the Sixth Constitutional Amendment, each and every person has the right to a jury trial and to have opposing witnesses appear in person. The only way we could get away with using your taped testimony exclusively would be if you were totally indisposed. Don't worry, though—we'll have plenty of time to prepare before the trial." DA Knower hit the "RECORD" button and I took the oath.

"Please state your name and county of residence."

"Rena Lorence—Schoharie County."

"What is your occupation?"

"I'm an animal rehabilitator and physical therapist."

"Where do you work?"

"I work in clients' homes, animal shelters and veterinary hospitals, as well as provide educational seminars at pet stores."

"How do you know Ralph Walway?"

"I was hired by Mr. Walway to treat his aging Great Dane—Moose."

"How long were you employed by Mr. Walway?"

"Approximately five weeks."

"As a physical therapist, what was your assessment of Mr. Walway's physical condition?" DA Knower stopped the tape and said, "We'll get an objection with that question since you were there to see the dog and not Mr. Walway, but I'll be able to convince the judge to overrule." He pushed "RECORD."

"Mr. Walway was always in a wheelchair. On my first visit, he advised me he was paraplegic. He said he had sustained a partial spinal cord injury in a hunting accident. He demonstrated that he could ambulate with a walker for short distances, but claimed it was extremely difficult. I had observed, however, that he had very good muscle tone and bulk in his lower extremities. I was skeptical of his proclaimed disability."

"Did Mr. Walway ever leave his apartment while you were treating his dog?"

"Yes—he left each time."

"How many times a week did you visit at the Walway residence?"

"I visited two to three times a week."

"Where did Mr. Walway say he was going?"

"He usually said he was going to see his mother and do errands."

"Do you know how he got around town?"

"Yes—he drove his car."

"Did he have special hand controls for his vehicle?"

"No, he didn't. I looked in his car windows one day as I was walking past so I could see his setup, but there were no special controls."

"Did Mr. Walway park in a handicapped-accessible space at his apartment building?"

"Not all of the time. I had observed his car on the side of the building near an emergency exit on at least two occasions."

"Was that because his usual spot had been taken?"

"No, his usual spot was free and there were plenty of other spots much closer to the main entrance."

"How did Mr. Walway usually exit the apartment building?"

"He had elevator access to the main lobby entrance."

"Was there an elevator accessible to him on the side of the building at the emergency exit?"

"No, there wasn't. I checked."

"Did you notice anything else unusual about that emergency exit when Mr. Walway had parked there?"

"Yes. I noticed one time that there was a videotape propped under the door to hold it open. Mr. Walway had driven off, so I retrieved the tape for him and closed the door. The emergency doors are supposed to be kept closed."

"What did you do with the tape then?"

"Since I had finished my treatment with Moose and no longer had the key to the apartment, I took the tape home."

"Did you watch the tape?"

"I did."

"What was on the tape?"

"There were various scenes. One was of a CVS store clerk with the name tag 'Sandy.' Most of that footage was on Sandy's breasts. The other scenes were of Mr. Walway having sex with various women in his bedroom."

DA Knower again stopped the tape and said there would be several objections along this line of questioning, but he was secure with it. "RECORD."

"How did you know it was Mr. Walway's bedroom?"

"Because Mr. Walway requested that I work with Moose on his bed for the dog's comfort."

"In your opinion, did Mr. Walway's paraplegia disable him in any way with his sexual performance?"

"No—as a matter of fact, he did not appear to be paralyzed at all, as he was able to assume a variety of positions."

"Did you see him stand unassisted?"

"Not in that particular videotape, but, yes, in another tape."

"Where did you find another tape?"

"There were several tapes, actually. They were in Mr. Walway's storage unit."

"What were you doing in Mr. Walway's storage unit?"

"I was let in to storage by another tenant, who showed me where to disengage the emergency-exit alarm, as I wanted to assess Moose on the stairs. I knew Mr. Walway had shut the alarm the day I found the tape propping the door. I decided to just return the tape to the storage unit since I was in there. That's when I found the other tapes."

"How many other tapes were there?"

"Oh, I don't think I could really say. They were stacked on about six shelves the length of the storage unit. I would think close to a hundred."

"What else did you find in the storage unit?"

"There was a video camera set up on a tripod against the far wall. The 'record' light was on. I looked through the viewfinder and saw Mr. Walway's bedroom. I was stunned to think that he had been recording my sessions with Moose. I grabbed a few more tapes and left."

"What did you find on those tapes?"

"Mr. Walway—engaged in more sexual acts. He seemed to be very much into S&M."

"Sado-masochism?"

"Yes. He seemed to enjoy sexual perversion. He also had a whip. I recognized one of the women as Sandy, the clerk from the CVS scene. Mr. Walway whipped her and she begged him to stop. He beat her and she fell through a door into the bathroom. She appeared to be unconscious. Mr. Walway then turned to face the camera and gave a thumbs-up sign. He left the room and a few seconds later, the film stopped."

"How did you know it was Mr. Walway's bathroom where the woman fell?"

"I knew it was the bathroom because he had forbidden anyone to enter it. I and *anyone* else providing care was instructed by him to use the bathroom in the lobby."

"Did you think that was an odd request?"

"Extremely odd and inconvenient. After viewing the tape of the beating, my curiosity got the best of me. I went back to the storage unit one day to turn off the camera and then returned to his apartment."

"What did you do then?"

"I was careful not to touch anything. I used tissue to open the bathroom door and flip the light switch."

"What did you see?"

"I saw what appeared to be blood stains on the walls near the toilet and sink. The shadow of the stain by the sink appeared to be a partial handprint. I became very scared, grabbed Moose and ran out of there. That's when I ran into Sophie Williams, Sandy's sister. She told me Sandy had been missing for a few days and she had found a message on Sandy's answering machine left by Mr. Walway. That's why she was there. She was looking for her sister. I asked her to leave with me and that's when we contacted my friend, Judge McGillacuddy and came to see you for help."

"STOP."

"Very good, Rena. When it comes close to the day of the trial, we'll review this tape so it will be easy for you to recall every detail…"

Chapter 65

Miller was surprised to find a couple of uniforms at the Derrows' when he tried to pull in the driveway. He backed out and parked down the street by a row of cedar trees. The front door to their home had been left wide open. Miller donned a pair of gloves, walking in cautiously, badge exposed. "What's going on here?"

"We got a call from a couple of Girl Scouts claiming that Mr. Derrow invited them in and told them to help themselves to this." He led Miller into the dining room. Strewn across the table was a fortune in jewelry. "They reported Derrow was crying and carrying on. Guess they were afraid someone might come in and clobber the guy."

"I guess they did their good deed for the day," Miller said. "Where's Derrow now?"

"He's in here." Again, Miller was led to another room, a breakfast nook where Derrow sat in his bathrobe and slippers, grumbling something unintelligible to himself. Miller squatted in front of him.

"Mr. Derrow—I'm Miller Sampson with BCI. I'm here to ask you some questions about your wife."

"Selma? Where is she? I keep calling for her—where the hell is she?"

"She's dead, Mr. Derrow. She died a few days ago."

"Oh, my God—she's dead! She's in the garden now with all the others." Then he calmly asked, "What day is it? Where's Selma?"

Miller slowly stood, quietly leaving Derrow alone with his mental chaos and joined the others. "He's delusional. Call Capital Psych—he needs protection."

The uniforms called for an ambulance, which arrived in record time. When one of the EMTs spotted the empty booze bottles scattered about and heard Louis' blathering, he said, "Korsakoff's psychosis, no doubt. No memory and confabulation—makes up stories."

Their heads all turned in synchrony to look at Louis, who casually asked, "What day is it? Where's Selma?"

They gently escorted him out of the house. Miller dismissed the uniforms but asked that they do the honors of locating and notifying next of kin. He decided to stay and have a look around as was his original intention. He told the others he'd secure the premises.

Miller made his way past the jewelry-laden dining area and ascended to the second floor. The bedrooms looked like they hadn't been used in a while—beds were neatly made, clothes hung, bathrooms clean. He entered what appeared to be an office where a wheel-based desk chair had fallen on its side like a child at a roller rink. Alongside the chair lay a lone crumpled piece of paper, no wastebasket remotely near. Smoothing its creases, Miller read:

> *Dear Louis. I can't go on like this. I'm losing my mind.*
> *I can't bear to see Bernard go through this anymore.*
> *There's nothing I can do to help him. It's out of our control*
> *now. You'll be taken care of—not to worry—Love, Selma.*

"Jesus—Selma committed suicide." Miller slipped the note in an evidence bag. As he scanned the sparsely furnished room, his eyes rested on a woman's framed photograph. 'That must be Selma,' he thought and then it hit him—he recognized her. 'The woman in the CVS surveillance video.'

195

Miller was startled when he heard footsteps downstairs.

"Hey, Derrow! Where the hell are you? I want my final payment. You still owe me half—remember?"

Miller drew his weapon and quietly moved toward the stairs.

"Hey, Derrow—maybe I'll just scoop up some of this jewelry. C'mon, man—where the hell are you?"

Miller could see the top of the man's head through the railing as he made his way up to the landing. Miller made one quick move to the top of the stairs. "***FREEZE!***"

Their eyes locked.

"*Miller!*"

"Gus?"…

Chapter 66

I really felt I was taking way too much on lately. Though my home clients had dwindled, I kept a full schedule at the shelters and hospitals. Today had just been ridiculously long, getting home at 8 p.m. I could barely get through my yoga class. I could hear Ed joking with a guest when I walked in. "Honey—I'm home," I sung out from the mudroom.

"Hey, baby doll. We're in the dining room. Gus is here—he's staying tonight. We already ate—can I get you something?"

"Well, I *see* you already ate," observing the scraps on their plates as I entered the dining room. I leaned over to kiss Ed. "No, sweetie, I'm going in the hot tub for a while and then I've got some paperwork to do. I'll eat when I'm done."

"I'll put a martini in the freezer for you," Ed cooed.

"I knew I married you for a good reason."

He and Gus laughed.

I finished my paperwork around 10 p.m., grabbed my frosted martini and started to fix myself a bite.

"You're still all pruny," Ed yawned. "I'm exhausted. I must have had

197

one glass of wine too many. Gus already went up to bed. I'm going, too—g'night." Ed kissed me through another yawn and headed upstairs.

Moose was already sacked for the night, too, and sawing wood as usual.

I wolfed my dinner and continued to savor my drink when I heard a faint voice say, "Don't be scared—don't be scared." It was Gus. "Sorry, I didn't want to startle you so thought I'd whisper my way into the room. I'm not sure why but I just can't get to sleep," he said, looking mildly perturbed.

"Don't you hate it when that happens?" We laughed. "You know, I'm not tired anymore either, Gus—why, I have *no* idea. You wanna have a drink with me?"

"Sure, Rena—I'd enjoy that."

"Mum's the word, though, Gus. I'm usually only a one-drink-a-night kind of a girl."

"You got it."

"I think I'll go get snug in my jammies first. I'll be down in a few minutes."

"Then let me have the honor of making your drink, Rena. It'll be ready and waiting when you come back down."

When I returned to the kitchen, Gus handed me my drink and we toasted to friendship. We sat in the den by the gas-fired stove and chatted a while about non-stress topics—weather, gardening, birds and such. Halfway through my second drink, I was suddenly overcome with exhaustion. 'Must have been the soak in the hot tub,' I thought. I downed the rest of the drink—'waste not, want not'—and said good night...

Chapter 67

Gus Freeman pulled a weapon and fired, shaving Miller's flesh just above the collarbone. Miller retaliated with a clean shot to the thigh. Gus dropped. Miller rode the stairs to the landing on his heels in a dream-like maneuver, flipping Gus to his belly like a rag doll to cuff him. Miller called for backup and an ambulance. This news would make Elisha Looby's day, Miller thought.

Gus's arrest coincided with a phoned-in complaint from Armando and Alena D'Jaccarina. They had reported to local authorities the vulgar smell coming from the Derrow garden and the strange man in the yard they spied the day before. On top of the arrest and complaint, Miller's discovery of the suicide note provided more than sufficient justification for a full search both inside and outside the Derrow premises.

Freeman was placed into custody and hauled away by ambulance. Miller's grazing was not life threatening. EMTs patched him up temporarily and he promised he'd have his wound tended to as soon as possible.

Investigators arrived and the search began. Outside, it didn't take the crew long to discover the reported stench. They started to dig. In just under two feet of topsoil and mulch, there it was—rotting flesh. An hour and fifty feet more of shoveled surface dirt later, five more bodies were uncovered. Miller wandered about the large, private, fenced plot of land, wondering how many more bodies would be found. As the others continued the mass exhumation, Miller made his way to the tool shed. He just stood there shaking his head as he scanned the various bottles and cans along the shelf of insecticides, herbicides and rodenticides. 'Now where the hell is the curare?' he asked himself.

Meanwhile, the inside search came up with an under-the-bed storage box, filled with newspaper clippings related to missing women, along with various drivers' licenses, ID badges, name tags, jewelry and eyeglasses, more than likely connected to the uniquely planted garden beds.

Miller left them to their work and decided to head to the hospital to have his wound looked at. The ER doc cleaned him up and gave him a couple of prescriptions. Gus had required surgery, as Miller had shattered his femur with perfect aim. Miller slept in the waiting area until Gus's surgeon gave him the okay to begin questioning.

"So, Gus—what role are you taking on today?"

"Well, Miller—I suppose it had to catch up with me eventually. I must admit, I'm too tired to keep this going. If you really want to know, my real name is Barney Davison. I'm just a starving actor trying to make a buck. I would never get any roles using my real name."

"So are you really a hit man or do you just play one on TV?"

"Listen—I'm not proud of what I did, but I needed the money and Derrow was willing to pay a pretty penny for knocking off that Lorence girl. I was kinda sad about that one, though. She seemed pretty decent."

"What the hell do you know about decency?"

"Well, compared to the others, I know a little. It was a lot easier to finish off the whores their son didn't have the guts to."

"Their son? Whose son?" Before Gus could answer, Miller's cell rang and he listened intently. "Holy shit—amazing. Yeah, right—thanks."

"So, Gus—I mean *Barney*—I just learned you aren't the only one with an alias in this case."

"Oh—you just got word, huh? Yeah, Derrow's son, Bernard—a.k.a. Ralph Walway. Did they find all the bodies yet?"

"They're still working on it. So, let me guess—the Derrows hired you to kill Rena because of what she knew?"

"Yeah—they didn't want her to testify at Bernard's trial."

"One more question—where'd you get the curare?"

"Oh, that was the easy part. I surfed the web and purchased the allowable amount online."

"And how did you get that last lethal dose into her?"

"Well, it was like this," Gus explained proudly. "I had planned to make it look like Ed was the culprit. I dosed Ed's wine with a couple of sedatives that night so that once his head hit the pillow, he was out for the count. I had scoured their place trying to find just the right spot to plant the curare after spiking Rena's second martini. I watched Ed earlier in the evening use a small key to open the face of a banjo clock in their dining room to wind it. When he locked it, I saw him hang the key from a small hook just under the clock. The curare must still be there. It's in a film case. Anyway, it was all very easy since Rena was already willing to have a second drink. I would have gotten it in her one way or other even if she hadn't."

"Unbelievable. Well, I guess it didn't go quite as swimmingly as you had hoped. Looks like *this* role came back to bite you in the ass—*no Oscar for you,*" Miller exclaimed in Seinfeld's Soup Nazi fashion.

Miller walked out of the room and clicked off his tape recorder. He called DA Knower. "It's confirmed, Al. We can add kidnapping and murder to Walway's convictions. I'll call Ed Lorence with the news…"

Chapter 68

Well, I could just shit a brick. Here I *prided* myself as being a good judge of character. Who-da-thunkit? Gus Freeman—I never would have guessed. He seemed so sincere. I would have thought someone like Nick or Marvin—but Gus? Never. Ralph, for sure—but not *Selma*. But, you know, I should have recognized that voice of hers in Ralph's CVS tape. I knew it sounded familiar. And no damn *wonder* I was always so tired and nauseous after visits with her and her at-the-ready baked goods. I just thought it was Louis' noxious personality wearing me down. Well, Ed will be relieved to get this over with. I bet he'll never invite any more strays to the house. Now he'll finally be able to get on with his life. I guess I'll be able to get on with mine, too. I'll have to take up a new hobby. Haunting sounds like it could be fun.

Gus Freeman—man, oh, man, you just never know…

Chapter 69

"Miller—it's Tiarra Smythe. I'm so glad it's over."

"You know? Tiarra—I must say—I don't think you need to second-guess yourself any more."

"I agree, Miller. I'm back in the groove."

"You were right all along about the key and the music—which happened to be related to the banjo clock. Plus the fact that you knew there was a woman behind it all and that Rena was in trouble because of what she *knew*. You really nailed it on the head and helped solve this case, you know, as well as the cold cases of all those missing women. I never believed in the supernatural before, but you've definitely changed my mind. I thank you from the bottom of my heart."

"It was my pleasure," Tiarra flirted. "By the way—how's your wound?"

"Wow, Tiarra—now you're really scaring me," Miller chuckled. "I'm a little weak in the shoulder. I think I'll need a little physical therapy."

"Maybe I can tune in to Rena and get you a good recommendation."

Miller drove to meet with Ed, Lydia and Blake. CSI was called in once again to bag the curare. They all listened in tears to Gus's crass taped confession. Ed just couldn't believe he'd been drugged that night and that the poison had been right there under his nose the whole time.

"I haven't wound that clock since the night of Rena's murder. I guess time just came to a dead stop for me after that."

"That's so amazing, Blake, that you dreamt of the banjo and took notice of that key in Rena's painting!" Lydia exclaimed.

"Well, how about you, Lydia? You dreamt about time running out and clocks!" Blake replied.

Miller advised them that my taped testimony had been heard in the Walway—now Derrow—case and it had a huge impact on the jury's decision. Miller also informed them that because the court had learned that my death was directly related to Ralph's trial, he would now be charged as an accessory in my murder as well. The jury would only have to decide between life in prison or the death penalty. "They will either continue to give him a free ride or fry him."

Ed looked at Lydia and Blake. "I'll call the coroner. We should be able to get Rena's ashes by the end of the week."

Lydia and Blake agreed to call the family and make their final arrangements.

Moose leaned hard into Ed's legs, looking at him with big, sad Moose eyes. "That's right, my boy—Rena's okay now—it's all over..."

Conclusion

"That's it," I said. "*The End*. Well? What did you think? How was it? C'mon –somebody say something!"

I had just completed a reading of my very first novel to my very patient family and dear friends, the McGillacuddys and Miller Sampson.

"So do you really plan to use our actual names?" Lydia asked.

"Sure, why not? You'll all be famous!"

"So do you really think that I'm 'downright handsome'?" Blake blushed.

"No doubt about it, baby bro!"

Miller was frank and to the point. "I like my character a lot. I think maybe George Clooney should play me in the movie version."

"Yeah, okay, Miller—I'll get right on that."

"Well then I want Meryl Streep to play me," MaryLou said and then scoffed, "and I'm really not all *that* quirky—hmph." Judge just smiled and poured her another cosmo.

"Well, Ed—you're being awfully quiet—aren't you going to comment?"

FAY ROWNELL

"Yeah, okay, but I'm a bit confused. Am I to take it, then, that you're really *not* dead?" Ed smirked.

"Why I *oughtta*," I chided as I fluttered my hand in front of Ed's face and playfully slapped his arm.

"What? Did I say something *wrong*?" he teased.

"No I'm *not* dead, silly. As a matter of fact, I'm just getting started!" We all raised our cocktail glasses—straight up—and enthusiastically toasted to my future writing career.

And with that Maggie glared at me, her dark eyes wide. Bristling her fur, she defensively arched her back and scornfully hissed.

Epilogue

…now exhale a sigh of relief
because—in the end—
it's all bullshit.

Printed in the United States
63120LVS00003B/97-99